THE SURGEON'S SCALPEL

THE SURGEON'S SCALPEL

HEINOUS CRIMES UNIT™ BOOK ONE

DANIEL SCOTT

Published by Marlowe & Vane
an imprint of LMBPN Publishing
PMB 196, 2540 South Maryland Pkwy
Las Vegas, NV 89109

Previously Published as *The Surgeon*
Version 1.01, September 2022
ebook ISBN: 979-8-88541-370-1
Print ISBN: 979-8-88541-720-4

THE SURGEON'S SCALPEL TEAM

Thanks to our Beta Readers
John Ashmore, Angela Wood, Rachel Beckford, Kelly O'Donnell, Mel Eagle, Alison Kelly, Daphne Reilly, Marty French

Thanks to our JIT Readers

David Laughlin
Alison Kelly
Daphne Reilly
Nat Roberts
Marty French

Editor

Lynne Stiegler

CHAPTER ONE

The madness started with a young man and a mute—as near as anyone could later pinpoint, anyway. Madness has a special way of hiding until, all at once, everyone can see it.

Charles Ranger had lost the ability to speak three years earlier, and every day since had been a special kind of hell. He wouldn't have wished this on his worst enemy, or at least that's what he'd thought when his ability to speak first left him. It had taken him three years, but he'd finally found someone that he wished could also carry this affliction.

Bradley Brown.

Charles Ranger was eighty-two years old, half-blind, mute, and living in a nursing home. The only thing he really had going for him was his hearing, but since meeting Bradley, he'd begun thinking he could go without that sense as well.

Bradley was one of the orderlies assigned to Charles' corridor. His kids had thrown him in here at seventy-five, and while they visited often, he hated the damn place. Or at least he'd thought he had, but once again, when he'd met Bradley, Charles had come to a different understanding of things.

Bradley stood behind his wheelchair, pushing him toward his room. It was time for Charles' afternoon nap, and although he rarely fell asleep, he would do anything to get away from the people in this place. Since he couldn't talk, the other old farts all decided they would talk to him. They babbled as Charles stared at the television screen. He had one of those boards he could write on, but it took so long, and none of the babblers cared when he tried communicating with it. He didn't even bother nodding anymore, didn't care one bit whether the other "inmates" thought he was rude.

"Well, Charlie," Bradley said, "here we are."

Charles hated *that* about Bradley Brown, too. The bastard kept calling him "Charlie."

The orderly opened the bedroom door and pushed him inside. He closed the door and then began helping Charles into his bed.

"I think it's about time for me to start what we've been discussing."

God, no. Please don't talk about it anymore, Charles thought. It had been two weeks since the last time Bradley brought it up, and Charles simply couldn't handle it anymore. He had to tell someone.

Who's going to believe you, old man? And if they do, and they investigate the bastard, what happens if they don't find anything? Bradley will know who told them. What do you think will happen to you then?

Charles had talked to himself about this multiple times already. It always ended with visions of him lying in bed and Bradley's tall body standing over him, holding a pillow with both hands.

"Should have kept it our little secret, Charlie," Bradley would say before pressing the pillow over Charles' face.

He couldn't tell anyone if he wanted to keep living.

"I've found the perfect girl. Finally. Her eyes, Charlie! If you could see them, you'd fall in love. Bright blue like the sky on steroids. I hope I can show them to you." He pulled the blankets up to Charles' chin. "I'm thinking sometime this week I'll do it. I can probably show you them the week after. You'll love 'em. I'm sure of it."

Charles looked up. Bradley was standing over him. The only thing missing was the white pillow he'd use to suffocate Charles.

"You're not going to tell anyone about this, right? I mean, you won't be writing any notes?"

Charles shook his head, wondering if the fear in his gut showed on his face.

"I didn't think so. I imagine you like it a little bit, don't you? Given what your profession used to be? I imagine cutting all those people up, even as a surgeon... Well, you had to enjoy the blood and guts, right?"

Charles nodded, although he hadn't focused on the blood when he'd been a surgeon, only on keeping his patients alive.

"That's why I came to you, Charlie. Because when I saw your patient file, I knew you were someone I could confide in. I can't wait to show you what I get."

Bradley turned and walked out of the room, leaving

Charles Ranger feeling certain that his closest caretaker was a serial killer.

Bradley Brown understood that sooner or later, he would kill Charlie Ranger. Not for his eyes, though. He had no desire for a man's eyes. No, he'd kill the old man because rules must be followed. Bradley was a big lover of rules and had been since his earliest memories.

He *needed* them.

Rules were the only reason he had made it this far in life. First his father's, then his own. If he was going to continue doing as he pleased, then he would need even more of them.

Because Bradley definitely was going to continue doing as he pleased. Doing what pleased *him*.

Rule Number 1: No witnesses. Charlie wasn't a witness, per se, but close enough, and sooner or later, he'd have to go. Hopefully later, because Bradley did enjoy talking to the old man. He bounced a lot of ideas off the bald guy's dome, and even though Charlie couldn't speak back, it clarified Bradley's thinking.

Clarity was important for what came next.

And goodness, Charlie served that purpose well.

At first, Bradley had thought about taking women he knew. They would be the easiest. He understood where they lived, their patterns, etc. Talking with Charlie had rid him of that notion. Well, talking and reading.

Bradley read *a lot*. He preferred a very specific genre: true crime with a focus on serial killers. He was, as far as he was concerned, the most knowledgeable person in the United States on the subject. If they gave out doctorates on the subject, Bradley would certainly have one.

Reading about the killer Ed Kemper had shown Bradley how foolish it would be to abduct people he knew. Ed had only killed hitchhikers until he got to his mother.

Bradley would read, and then he'd talk to Charlie. In the end, his plan developed into something nearing perfection. *He* wouldn't be caught, not like Ed or Jeffrey or Ted.

Ed had turned himself in.

Jeffrey had been caught because he was a fucking idiot. Same with Ted.

The cops, in every case, had been about as clueless as anyone could possibly be. In Jeffrey Dahmer's case, they had sent an underage boy who had a hole in his head filled with acid *back* to Dahmer. Old Jeffrey had told them they were boyfriends and the underage boy was drunk. Believable enough.

Ted Bundy had escaped from jail.

Escaped. From. Jail.

When Bradley realized that, it had taken a few minutes to sink in. The police, the FBI, they were all so incompetent that Bradley could do whatever he wanted, as long as he followed his rules. Truthfully, the fear of incarceration or the death penalty had been the only thing that kept Bradley from doing it sooner.

That was over now, though.

Bradley's parents had his IQ tested as a boy, putting him at 145, which was in the upper echelon.

He was far too smart to be caught by people who would

send someone with a *goddamn hole in his head* back to a cannibalistic serial killer.

No, it was time to start.

———

Crystal thought Liam was cute for someone in this bar.

Doesn't matter. Not like he ever hits on you.

Liam had started coming to Crystal's restaurant and the Happiest Hour about six weeks ago. He always came in late in the evening, when the bar had slowed down and the servers were beginning to clean their sections. He sat at the bar and drank a few beers while eating chips and salsa. He never ordered anything, and it wasn't until the second week that he really started talking to Crystal.

"How often are you up here?" she asked as she put down a new basket of chips.

"Four or five nights a week."

"Don't want to go home?"

Liam smiled, which was when he was at his cutest. "I'm trying not to become an alcoholic. I feel drinking at home and eating chips out of a bag instead of a basket in a restaurant classifies me as one."

"The basket is the line that separates you from them?" she asked, smiling as well.

"The basket and this place. They keep me at a safe distance from any classifications."

"Oh, goodness." She laughed. "I'm going to take a smoke break, okay? Need anything before I run out back?"

"Nope, I'm good."

Crystal walked through the kitchen, heading to the employees' entrance. She stepped outside.

"Aw, hell," she said.

The rain was pouring down, and the alley was starting to flood. Crystal pulled the pack of smokes from her pocket and lit one, careful not to step off the small stoop with the overhang above it. She watched the rain fall and worried about how little money she'd made this week.

She wasn't going to get the car, not this month. She would need an awesome weekend of tips just to make rent. And the goddamn Ubers were eating into her tips pretty heavily. It was a cycle she couldn't escape, not by bartending here, anyway.

Fuck it, she thought and flicked the cigarette onto the soaked concrete.

Crystal walked back into the bar, trying to push her current financial predicament away. Pouting wouldn't bring in any extra tips, that was for sure.

"Rain's really coming down," Liam said, staring up at the television behind the bar.

"Yeah. Makes getting in an Uber even harder."

"What do you mean?" he asked.

"Well, I'm not getting in the car with just anyone that pulls up to the curb. I always check to make sure their license plate matches what the app says."

"You gotta do that, even in this rain?"

"It's either that or risk being cut up into little pieces."

The small smirk. "True. What time do you get off?"

"About thirty minutes after closing time. As soon as Bill checks me out."

"I could give you a ride tonight, save ya the trouble of checking license plates," Liam said.

Oh, wow, is he finally hitting on me?

Don't be silly. He's offering you a ride home so that you don't have to stand in the rain. He's being nice.

"I don't want to make you do that," Crystal said. "I'll be fine."

"It's really no problem. Let me finish this beer, I'll go fill up with gas, and by the time I'm back, you should be just about done, okay?"

Liam looked from the television to her, and Crystal wanted to say yes. It would save her twenty bucks and keep her out of the rain...and she wanted to hang out with him a little longer.

"You're sure?"

"Sure, I'm sure," he said.

"Okay."

Bradley could have stared at Crystal Hembree's eyes forever. In fact, that's what he planned to do. He'd told Charlie he knew it would happen soon, but he hadn't thought the opportunity would present itself *this* quickly.

Bradley wasn't going to look a gift horse in the mouth, though.

He did as he'd said, or as Liam had said. He finished his beer, went and put gas in his car, then pulled up to the front of the restaurant. The rain was torrential, which was good. Now that everything was in motion, he didn't know if he could shut it down if she decided to use an Uber because the rain stopped.

Bradley hadn't asked for her number, just said he'd be out front. Even if she gave it to him, he wouldn't text her. That would have been dumb. No records would connect him and Crystal. At best, her boss might know a guy named Liam had taken her home.

Five minutes passed before he saw her stick her head out the front door, holding a jacket over it.

Bradley flashed his lights, and she rushed across the concrete. He pushed open the passenger door, and she dove in.

"Thanks so much," she said, water dripping from her jacket. Her blue eyes met his, and Bradley understood that he would have done anything for them. To just stare into them anytime he wanted, for the rest of his life.

***

"Who called it in?" Tommy Phillips asked.

"A maintenance man. The smell finally made its way through the walls, I suppose. Someone complained and when maintenance entered the premises... Well, I suppose we'll see soon enough."

Tommy looked at Luke Titan. "You haven't been in yet?"

"No."

"What the hell have you been doing?"

"Waiting for you."

Tommy looked up at the apartment. The door was closed with no one around it. The police had sealed it off and referred the case to the FBI, which was happening more and more lately. Anything they didn't want to deal with, *especially* crimes of grotesque natures, they referred to the Heinous Crimes Unit.

It was, in Tommy's opinion, getting a bit ridiculous.

Not every death that didn't have a simple bullet wound to the head made it a heinous crime and worthy of FBI attention.

"Well, let's head on up."

The two took the stairs, Tommy pulling his small notepad out and Luke carrying nothing as usual. The man never wrote a thing down, and Tommy envied it. He envied a lot about Luke, but then again, so did most people.

Two yellow banners formed an X over the door, reading: POLICE LINE DO NOT CROSS.

Tommy reached up and carefully pulled at the top of each banner, letting them float down to the ground.

"You smell it?" he asked, knowing he didn't need to.

"Yes," Luke said.

Tommy understood Luke's speech patterns now, though it'd taken him roughly six months as partners. The man talked like a professor, one who had been educated at the finest institutions. Indeed, he spoke like someone who had been born two hundred years ago as an English noble. Luke told Tommy at one point that Americans had so successfully butchered the English language that he thought the country should start calling their version "American."

Both men pulled on sterile gloves and booties, after which Tommy turned the doorknob and pushed.

The lights were off, and the clouds outside the apartment kept much sunlight from entering.

Tommy stepped inside but didn't turn the lights on, not wanting to smudge any fingerprints on the switch. They would rely on the sunlight filtering through the windows for now.

"Jesus," he said.

Luke was quiet.

The victim's head sat on the kitchen counter. Blood had dried across the counter. It had also dripped down to the floor, where it pooled.

Tommy reached into his pocket and pulled out the vapor rub all agents carried for crime scenes like this. He rubbed it under his nose but didn't bother to offer Luke any. All agents *except* Luke carried it. The smell of rotting corpses never seemed to bother his partner.

Tommy moved across the living room to the kitchen, staring at the severed head. "Her eyes are missing."

Luke was quiet, but Tommy heard him move to the couch on the right wall. Tommy turned and saw where the rest of the body sat.

On the sofa, arms spread out over the back as if the woman was simply sitting there watching a television show, except without a head.

Tommy squatted some, putting him eye to eyeless with the head.

"He left her mouth open."

"Might not be a he," Luke said from the living room.

"Always the fucking feminist, aren't you?"

"Don't want to get tunnel vision. Perhaps it was a scorned lover, and our victim here was a lesbian."

Tommy flipped back a few pages in his notebook and started scribbling what he saw. He went quiet at this stage in the game, resembling Luke. He needed to focus, to catch every detail. Luke's success in this business, as in every business he'd ever been in, stemmed from his intelligence. Tommy's, however, came from his work ethic.

He peered into the mouth and saw that the tongue had been removed. Something else was inside.

"Jesus," Tommy said again. An eyeball was lodged in the victim's throat. "We need to call FBI forensics in STAT."

"Give me a minute, though, please, before we invite them."

Tommy knew what that meant. He stood and went to the living room where Luke was.

The body was naked, and the legs had been crossed. While her breasts were visible, her genitalia had been covered.

"That was nice of him," Tommy said.

"Or her."

Luke sat down on the couch next to the corpse, under one of the arms. Something else Tommy was used to, the morbidity with which the man worked. He was, of course, careful not to disturb anything. His movements were performed with a precision Tommy thought Michael Jordan would appreciate.

"What did the eyeholes look like? Was there a lot of hacking involved, or is it pretty neat?"

"Neat," Tommy said. "The eyeball he left in her mouth is intact."

"Our killer didn't take as much time with the head. He sawed on it hard and rough. You can see it from the multiple cut wounds where he started at least twice. He used a saw, not an ax."

Tommy looked over the torso, seeing that Luke was right.

He knew what came next. Luke Titan's genius. The reason for his rapid rise. *Insight.*

"Motive?" Tommy asked.

Luke didn't look away from the body but leaned closer. He put his nose to the woman's savaged neck and inhaled. Tommy felt his stomach threatening to turn. Even after a year of working with the man, he still grew sick at this part. He didn't ask why Luke did it, though. He had once, and the answer had been simple: *sometimes you can still smell their soul.* He hadn't smiled as he said it.

Finally, after a large breath, Luke turned and looked at Tommy.

"I'm not sure yet. The cops, though, were right to call us. This may be his first, but it won't be his last."

CHAPTER TWO

Christian Windsor looked into his phone, the front-facing camera showing him exactly what he thought was happening.

His tie.

His freaking tie.

He could never get the knot right. Had *never* been able to, and the damn thing looked ridiculous.

"It looks stupid," he said, not noticing the woman sitting next to him on the train. "Ridiculous, ridiculous, ridiculous."

There wasn't time to redo it. He had four minutes until his stop, then seven and a half minutes to cross the two blocks to the FBI headquarters.

"This is bad. So bad."

The woman slowly turned her gaze back to her own phone.

Christian put his eyes down and did his best to keep his thoughts from venturing back to his tie.

Your thoughts don't control you, Melissa said. He saw her standing on the train, holding on to one of the poles. Of course, Melissa wasn't there. His psychiatrist was in her office, probably helping other patients, but it was still comforting to see her. To hear her words.

Comfort is good for everyone, his mom said, her voice coming from a few seats back. Christian didn't turn around to look at her because he knew that wouldn't go over well with others on the train.

Comfort. My thoughts don't control me. Take solace in comfort. He repeated the words inside his head, trying his best to push the damned tie knot away.

The train arrived at his stop, and he stepped off. He didn't need a map to know where he was heading, though it was the first time he'd been there. He had memorized Washington DC's roads and train lines years ago and still knew them as well as the rooms in his mother's house.

"Except for the new ones," he added aloud. "They're always building new ones. That's why I regularly check them."

No one paid any attention to the young man speaking to himself as he walked up the left side of the metro's escalators. It was October, so there weren't many tourists in the city. Tourists knew nothing about escalator etiquette. You always *stood* on the right and let those needing to walk go left. Christian thought a businessman in wingtip shoes might slit some tourist's throat one day for standing on the escalator's left side.

He reached the crosswalk in front of the building he needed. Three and a half minutes. He'd make it.

Christian was very concerned with punctuality.

He entered the building, showed his badge at the front desk, and then his nervousness started. He didn't want to be here. In fact, he regretted every decision he'd made in the past two years, starting with the decision to apply to the FBI.

"An analyst," he said. "I wanted to be a freaking analyst."

The security guard at the front desk looked up. "Excuse me?"

"Nothing. Just talking to myself."

A few more seconds passed before the guard handed him a temporary ID badge. "Go back to the right. Keep going. It's going to be a long walk. When you get to the elevator, there will be a security guard there. Show him your ID, then place this temporary one inside the elevator card reader. Once you do that, it'll let you off on the correct floor."

"Thanks," Christian said, already walking off. His mind was calculating the time it would take. Probably two and a half minutes, maybe a few seconds more on either side. It depended on the technical specifications of the elevator, as well as the floor it was currently on.

The panic rose in him with each step he took.

"Analyst, analyst, analyst," he repeated to himself.

He didn't look the next security guard in the eye. He just placed his badge in the elevator card reader, and sure enough, it started rising. *Ten seconds for the elevator,* he decided based on its ascension velocity.

And finally, he was where he didn't want to be.

In the director of the FBI's office.

Christian shook his head as he stepped off, knowing he didn't want to be here and that his tie was a mess.

"Hi, Mr. Windsor. Please have a seat. Director Waverly will be with you in a second."

Despite Christian's almost crippling panic, his mind did what it had always done and took in everything around him. The assistant was forty-two years old and had smoked at one time. Her teeth still held the stains, but her fingertips were no longer yellow. Her smile was genuine, reaching her eyes.

Christian knew that without concentrating on it. He would, of course, be able to recall the information if he ever needed it.

On the surface, Christian sat in a chair and continued obsessing over his tie.

Your tie is fine, Christian, Melissa said. She sat next to him, wearing a dark suit. He didn't look at her. That wouldn't be smart. Christian had learned, or rather, his mother had taught him, that the things he saw were his mind's way of helping him deal with stressful situations.

"It's okay to use them as tools," she'd told him when he was ten. "You just don't want other people to know that you're using them. there's nothing wrong with it, but other people might not understand."

That's what *Christian* understood: most people would never really understand him. His mother did. Melissa did. That was all he needed.

"Mr. Windsor?"

Christian looked up at the FBI's director. He knew the man's height and weight, as well as his curriculum vitae.

He didn't match his public picture, but those things were always taken with the subject's best look in mind. Alan Waverly had a paunch, though Christian doubted he was in serious danger of a heart attack. If the paunch continued growing, however, he would be one day.

"Hi. I'm Christian Windsor," he said, standing. The director extended his hand.

Christian looked at it for five seconds.

You have to, Melissa said from behind him.

He took the director's hand and shook it. "I'm sorry. I'm not great in social situations."

Alan Waverly smiled. "I've heard. Let's go back to my office and talk, okay?"

Christian nodded, dropping eye contact and following the man through the hallway. His peripheral vision allowed his mind to categorize what the corridors looked like without him having to glance around. He hated glancing around.

They reached the office, and the director walked over to a large conference table. Christian stopped once he entered.

"This is very nice. Much nicer than the cubicles I assume are on the rest of the floors."

The office was large, with pictures of the director alongside dignitaries littering the walls. Family photos sat on his desk next to a large monitor, though the screen was currently black.

Alan Waverly laughed. "Yes, I agree. I imagine they'd rather sit in something like this as well. Come take a seat."

Christian walked to the conference table and sat. "I

shouldn't have said that. I say things without thinking. My mom says I don't have a filter. My therapist says the same."

Nothing sat on the table, not a notepad nor a tablet for the director to take notes on.

What's that mean? he wondered.

"Well, Christian, I know a bit about you. You wouldn't be at this meeting, especially before becoming a full-fledged FBI agent, if I didn't. I know about your idiosyncrasies. I'll tell you when you need to apologize for something you've said, so no need to until then, okay?"

"Okay," Christian said, staring at the shiny wooden table before him. That was one thing Christian never had any interest in, decorations, so he knew nothing of the wood, only that it looked extremely nice.

"Now, do you know why you're here?"

"Professor Gauge recommended you meet me. He said he thinks that it would be good for me to get into field work. I don't want to do field work, Mr. Director."

"Call me, Alan, please," he said, still smiling. Christian wondered if the smile was genuine or if it was simply a politician's tool, much like the mask Christian used to get him through the day. "Yes, your professor did end up getting in touch with me, though it took much longer than I would have liked. I've looked over your records. You're number one in your class at Quantico—"

"Not in the physical trials. I'm not good at those. I'm only in the middle of the pack," Christian interrupted without looking up.

"I know that, and the middle of the pack is fine. I'm not looking for an Olympic gold winner. I'm looking for someone with your *mental agility.* I don't want to beat around the bush here, Christian. I asked you to come because I have a very specific job offer for you, and truthfully, it's a great opportunity. You will be immediately moving up about five years in your career."

"What is it?" Christian asked, though he already knew. The director didn't call people to his office for an analyst position.

"Field work with a very special team. We have a division that deals with exceptional cases, crimes that involve deranged individuals, including serial killers. The team consists of two people. One is Thomas Phillips, and the other is Luke Titan."

The director stopped talking to let the second name sink in.

Luke Titan wasn't just known in the FBI. He was known throughout the world. Christian knew his age, of course—thirty-nine last month. He joined the FBI two years ago, having skipped Quantico. He'd been the first person to ever do it, and the President of the United States had had to approve the request.

Luke Titan had started college at thirteen, completing a medical doctorate as well as a Ph.D. in astrophysics. Christian, not to mention the rest of the world, couldn't fathom why he had joined the FBI, especially given what he'd accomplished in his other careers.

"I think you would be a great addition to the team," Waverly said, "and I'd like to offer you a spot on it. They're stationed in your hometown, too. Atlanta."

Christian started shaking his head. "I wanted to be an

analyst. I signed up to be an analyst, not for fieldwork. I'm not good at meeting people. I don't like groups. I don't like traveling. I don't like any of it."

"I know. Professor Gauge told me about your resistance. He also told me why you joined the FBI. Your resume would not naturally lead to us, with your dual graduate degrees in theoretical physics and psychology.

"You have a unique ability to understand others *and* deal with complex numbers. You could be making a lot of money at any university in the world or consulting for almost any firm. Instead, you chose the FBI. Gauge told me, but I'd like to hear it from you. Why did you sign up for Quantico?"

Christian stopped shaking his head and finally looked up at the director. "I-I don't want to say."

"That's fine, but it doesn't mean you're not going to. We don't have to start there, though. Tell me about the dual degrees."

Christian closed his eyes. He didn't turn inward; there was no need for that here. He wanted darkness to surround him because he was being forced to open up. He knew that following these directions was imperative if he wanted a career when he left this office.

"The smartest minds in the world are figuring out how to get people to click ads. I have a tough time connecting with people, though I want to. My mom doesn't have that problem. She can connect with anyone, and I saw how much of a difference she made for people. I can't do that, ever, but I think there are very severe problems facing the world, and if I could address those problems, maybe I could help people like she did, albeit indirectly. I didn't want to do that by getting people to click ads."

"Good. Now tell me why the FBI."

Christian swallowed, still not opening his eyes. He didn't bother to think about what it looked like to the director that he was sitting in this massive office with his eyes shut during a meeting. The panic would be too much.

"I-I'm twenty-three. I'm smart. I'm very smart. I thought working with the FBI would allow me to have a quicker impact, and I could spend ten years or so here helping those who are suffering. Then, when I'm in my thirties, I could start working on large-scale problems."

"But you signed up to be an analyst?"

"Yes," Christian replied. "I don't like being around people. I don't like meeting people. I like numbers. I like spreadsheets."

"Christian, analysts are important in our line of work, but they're a dime a dozen. Any college kid with a finance degree can analyze what we need, and for the tough ones, we have doctorates in statistics and the other mathematical sciences that I have no clue about. If you're here to help, and you really want to do some good, *you* need to be in the field. You need to be looking at crime scenes so that we can catch criminals. Not crunching numbers."

Christian opened his eyes and stared across the table, though he knew Melissa stood next to him.

If you walk out of here, your career is over. You always talk about wanting to be like your mom. Here's your chance, she said.

He shut his eyes tight so that creases formed in the corners. "For how long?"

"The job contract will be for a year. After that, you'll be as free as a bird."

"If I don't take it, Director Waverly, I've just wasted two years at Quantico, haven't I?"

"I don't know about wasted," the director said, "but you certainly won't reach your potential here."

CHAPTER THREE

"I did it," Bradley said.

Charles closed his eyes and wished for death. This couldn't be happening. The orderly had to be messing with him, playing a prank that he'd go back and tell his friends about.

I got this old fart at work believing I'm a murderer. He's scared shitless!

"It was... God, it was good, Charlie. I can't even tell you how it felt, not really. It's something you have to *experience.* Was that what surgery was like for you? Was there any way to actually *describe* it?"

Charles shook his head. His eyes were still closed. The orderly had come to get him after his nap and was now taking him to the common area.

This was a joke. It had to be.

"I froze one of her eyes last night. I'll figure out how to bring it in here to show you, but I can't just yet. I need to make sure I keep it frozen. I'm sorry, Charlie. I know you wanted to see it, too."

Charles opened his eyes. Thank God, they had arrived. Bradley would have to shut the fuck up.

"I'll be back with your food in a little bit. Is this okay, in front of the television?"

Charles nodded.

The orderly patted his shoulder as he walked away. Charles could almost feel slime where Bradley touched him, a poison the pat had transferred to him.

Betty Lewis was already heading for Charles, having seen the damned orderly from a mile off. Ready to start gabbing, not caring in the slightest that Bradley Brown had just confessed to *murder*.

"How are ya, Charles?" the old hag asked.

Charles stared at her.

"You don't look well," the hag continued. "You look like you've just seen a ghost! Did I ever tell you about the time my sister saw a ghost? She must have been..."

Charles didn't look at the television. He didn't turn away from Betty. He stared at the old hag while she spoke, not hearing a word.

He thought about nothing but Bradley's words. The psychopath had started killing, and Charles couldn't tell anyone without dying himself.

Christian shook his head in short bursts. He wasn't sitting in front of the FBI's director now but his therapist, Dr. Melissa Keens. Well, not in front of her since they were using their computers to video chat. Since he'd come to Virginia, he couldn't travel home for his sessions, but he sure as hell wasn't getting another therapist.

"You're doing it again," she told him.

"I know." Christian didn't stop shaking his head.

"What did you tell the director?"

"That I needed a night to think about it. I asked for a night. A night's not long enough, though, not nearly. I don't want to do this, Melissa. I don't want to work for that man or his serial killer group or even the FBI."

Melissa was quiet. If she had heard her patient call her by her first name, she didn't say anything, nor had she the other five hundred times Christian had done it. Everyone else called her Dr. Keens, but not Christian.

"What did your mom say about it?"

"I didn't tell her."

"Because you know what she'll say, don't you?" Melissa asked.

"Do you take pleasure in describing the rope that's tied around my neck?"

Melissa smiled. "A little. Christian, your mother will say you have to take this chance. If you think about it, how many other people in Quantico would kill you...literally *kill* you...to have this opportunity that has been placed in your lap?"

"I don't know. I haven't thought about how many psychopaths are in my class. Based on statistics, five would kill me."

"How many, based on statistics, are envious?"

Christian didn't say anything. He knew what she was getting at. He had a chance the vast majority of people would never receive.

"I'd like to know why you're scared of fieldwork," Melissa asked. "Why are you so against it?"

He finally quit shaking his head and looked at her on the computer screen. "You're the shrink. Don't you know?"

"Maybe, but I'd like to hear you say it."

"Because I'm not good around people." His words were short and clipped. "I hate you right now, you know? And because I couldn't help but say *that* is the exact reason I don't want this job. I want to look at spreadsheets. I want to profile killers and write reports about them. I *do not* want to look at crime scenes, no more than I want to be looking at you right now."

His psychiatrist didn't twitch at his harsh words. "You can close your computer, Christian. No one makes you meet with me, and no one can make you take that job, but doing the right thing is rarely easy. It's the easy decisions we repeatedly make that lead to the outcomes we do not want."

"I'm sorry." Christian looked at his feet. "I didn't mean it."

"I know. So, what are you going to do?"

"I guess I'm going to take the job."

"Good, because *I* would kill you if you didn't," Melissa stated.

Luke Titan sat next to his partner in the director's office. Luke didn't like Alan Waverly and thought he would like to kill him one day. He knew it could be accomplished, but the time hadn't yet come.

To Luke, Alan Waverly had risen to his current position for political reasons and not merit. Tommy, his partner, had risen through the ranks due to hard work and a talent for deductive reasoning. Alan Waverly, though, was a politician. A poor man's version of Bill Clinton, despite how high he'd risen.

"The kid is different," Waverly continued. He'd flown Luke and Tommy up here to tell them about the new addition, which was serious in and of itself. "He hasn't been diagnosed, but the people that know him best say he's a high-functioning autistic."

"With all due respect, sir, why do you think he should be put on our team?" Tommy asked from Luke's left.

Waverly looked at Luke. "You have any idea?"

He always tested Luke to see if he knew things he shouldn't. Things that hadn't yet been handed down from on high.

"No, sir," Luke said. He lied to the director every chance he got. Luke wasn't concerned with what society said about him as long as it said the right things, and it had done so for the past two decades. If Luke moved too quickly, he could cause the world to start saying things he didn't want to hear, and *that* wouldn't be good.

Waverly nodded and looked at Tommy. "His inability to form connections with other people doesn't mean he can't *understand* other people. In fact, his tests show that his emotional intelligence quotient is one of the highest we've seen at Quantico. He is a genius on Luke's level."

"Yes, sir," Tommy replied.

Luke's face didn't change after the director's last

sentence, but the words rang loudly inside his head like a bell whose rope was being repeatedly pulled.

"He accepted the position this morning. He's starting tomorrow. I want him on this decapitation case, okay?"

"Yes, sir," Tommy replied.

"Yes, sir," Luke concurred, the bell clanging *too* loudly.

CHAPTER FOUR

Tommy looked at the young man and immediately understood what Waverly had meant about him being different. Tommy had only met the director twice before, both times involving promotions, with the final one occurring a year ago when he teamed Luke and Tommy up.

Now they were adding a third, and Tommy understood his feelings on the subject didn't matter. Luke had been silent, of course. The man never gave the world much as to what he thought, which was smart. Tommy did the same, especially when it came to orders from on high. You kept those thoughts to yourself lest someone else decided spreading *your* dislike could benefit *them.*

"So, this is everything we have," Tommy said. "The papers are calling him 'the Surgeon.'" The table in front of them was covered with photos of the crime scene. The three of them had flown to Atlanta the previous day, and they now stood in Luke's basement, though that didn't accurately describe the room. Perhaps "second house" was a better term. The place was huge, complete with plush furniture and a massive television. Pool table. Full bar.

Luke had done well for himself before joining the FBI.

They worked here for most of their cases, printing whatever photos were needed and connecting securely to the FBI servers as necessary. Luke liked working in his basement, and despite Tommy's original hesitation, he'd found he liked it, too.

Tommy used his computer for much of his work, but Luke didn't. He needed space to move, and when he got started, he liked to write on walls. The walls in the part of the basement they reserved for work were decked out with whiteboards.

They had asked Christian to come first thing this morning.

Standing above the table, he stared at the photos in front of him. He hadn't said more than two words since he'd shown up.

"It's probably going to be awkward at first," Tommy said, knowing that if he didn't offer the kid a lifeline, Luke wouldn't. "Luke and I have a way of working together. We're going to need to make some accommodations for you, but—"

"Where's the eye?" the kid interrupted.

Tommy's brows furrowed as he glanced at Luke. His partner shrugged.

"It's at the morgue with the rest of the body."

"We should go there," Windsor said. "When is the autopsy taking place?"

"Tomorrow, I believe."

"Can you get it pushed up to today?"

"Why?" Luke asked. It was the first question he had blessed the group with.

Windsor didn't look up. "There's something inside the eye."

"Why would you think that?" Luke asked.

"He took one and left one. The one he took was a present for himself. The one he left was a present for us."

"I shouldn't have said that, should I?" Christian asked the two when they stood in the front of the car.

"Said what?" Tommy asked from the driver's seat.

"I shouldn't have said we need to head to the morgue. I'm the new guy. I should be quiet and let you two decide, right?"

"No, you're fine," Tommy assured him. Christian heard the smile in the man's voice, understanding that his new partner thought him odd.

No one said anything else as the car pulled onto the highway.

Christian kept his eyes open, but if either Tommy or Luke looked in the rearview mirror, they would have seen them glaze over. Christian only knew what he looked like when he went inward because his mother had told him.

If you have to do it, do it in private, honey. People will think it's very different.

Normally he heeded her advice, but right now, he wanted to look at everything they had just shown him again.

Christian no longer saw the car. Instead, he stood in the

foyer of a massive mansion. Two staircases split fifty feet in front of him, one turning left and the other right in a half-spiral to the second floor of the building. From there, they would continue their spirals up ten floors, with massive wings jetting off to either side.

Christian began building the place when he was seven.

His mind needed somewhere to put the data it captured, and it captured *everything*. Whatever Christian heard, saw, or thought was categorized and placed in here. Most of it would never be needed again, but if it was, he could access it.

He already felt the new room being built. The construction was happening in the mansion's west wing. Christian took his time walking up the staircase. He had no taste for decoration, so his bare feet echoed off the stone that he'd laid down years ago. He thought once he finally had the time, he would study interior design some and decorate the place the way it deserved. For now, it was cold and utilitarian, the same as his brain.

He made his way to the new room. Other rooms sat across from it, as well as to the left and right, each one of them having a word or phrase etched above their door.

This room, the newest, simply said "Surgeon."

Christian walked through the doorway and into the room. The walls were digital, as were most of the rooms in his mind. Not much furniture filled the middle, but the pictures he'd been shown were now replicated perfectly across the walls. Christian turned around, wondering what else his mind might have put in here that he hadn't been consciously aware of during the briefing.

"Nothing yet," he said aloud. He walked across the

room to a thin pole protruding from the floor and rising to his face's height. An eyeball hovered over it, not touching anything. The missing one, not the eye they were heading to see. Its blue color had startled Christian when he first saw it, but his mind still captured and replicated it perfectly.

He didn't need to bend down to see it.

"Was it the blue you liked?" he asked. "Or just the eyes? Or is it both?"

Luke sat in the passenger seat of Tommy's car. The three of them drove in silence, with Tommy periodically trying to make conversation with the boy in the back. Luke definitely considered him a boy, despite whatever age his body showed. A boy, but a very smart one.

Luke had figured there would be something in the remaining eyeball, although he hadn't said anything about it yet. He would let the pathologist perform the autopsy.

Tommy, of course, hadn't known, and Luke didn't figure anyone else in the FBI would have thought of it either. Not by looking at the eyeball, certainly. There was only the slightest laceration at the very bottom of it, and the glue placing it back together was flawless. No one else saw it at the crime scene, and without a doubt, the boy hadn't seen it either.

Yet he knew.

This was something Luke hadn't planned on.

Waverly hadn't been lying about Windsor's intelligence. Luke did his own research the previous night, looking into

Windsor's past. It took a few hours, but eventually, he knew every standardized test Windsor had taken, as well as his scores. High-functioning autism was the correct diagnosis, with some doctors classifying it as Asperger's. Luke thought that was probably right, too. This boy differed from others with the same diagnosis in another way besides his intelligence: his emotional attention.

Windsor had known something he shouldn't have, simply by looking at crime photos. He'd known something *about* the criminal, something no one else had even guessed at.

This will be interesting, Luke thought as the car rolled on in silence.

***

"You think he's right?" Tommy asked as he and Luke walked to the restroom. They'd left the kid sitting in the "cutting room," waiting for Roger to come out of his office and start the autopsy. "You think there's something in the eye?"

Luke pushed the bathroom door open and went to the sink.

"There probably is."

"Why do you say that?" Tommy unzipped his fly, hearing Luke splash some water on his face.

"There was a small incision at the base of the eye. I saw it when Forensics was looking at it."

"You didn't feel it necessary to tell me?" Tommy asked, turning his head as far as he could over his shoulder.

"I figured if I was right, we would be told during the

autopsy. Forensics didn't see it, so I thought my eyesight might be going bad."

"I bet that's it," Tommy said, finishing up. He went to the sink and started washing his hands. He wasn't upset. He knew his partner's operating protocols. Luke rarely said anything until it was necessary to pull the rest of the group along. "He's smart, huh, this kid?"

"I'd say so."

"Smarter than you?" Tommy looked at Luke, grinning.

"What do you think?" Luke asked, flashing a smile.

He walked from the bathroom, leaving Tommy to finish washing his hands.

If he threw that grin around, he might get laid, Tommy thought as he grabbed a few paper towels.

Tommy followed Luke back to the cutting room and the metal table he'd seen over and over. Bodies came and went on the table. Tommy supposed he was similar to the table, unchanging when it came to bodies.

It was necessary for his job.

"Roger, this is Christian Windsor. He's new to our team," Tommy said as Roger walked into the room.

"Nice to meet you," the pathologist said without looking at the kid.

He went to the metal table and pulled back the white sheet draped over it. The body and head rested as they would have if no decapitation had occurred, except for the two-inch space separating them.

An eyeball lay next to the head.

"Okay." Roger slipped gloves over his hands. "We think there's something inside the eyeball. I took X-ray images earlier to make sure we weren't dealing with an explosive device, and while there isn't anything inside that can kill us, there *is* something."

The pathologist grabbed a small blade and picked up the eyeball. Luke, Christian, and Tommy stood around the table, with Roger at the head. Tommy looked at Christian, but the kid only stared at his shoes, not following the eyeball turning in Roger's hand.

He made his incision, cutting firmly and deep to open the membrane.

"Whoever did this drained it before putting anything inside," Roger said when no fluid emptied from the eye. Using his thumbs, he pulled open the incision. The inside was hollow, like a hardboiled egg without the yolk.

"Jesus," Roger said. Using tweezers, he pulled out something thin and small.

"What is it?" Tommy asked.

"It's a part of someone else's eye. He shaved off the iris and the pupil," Christian Windsor said, still not looking up from his shoes.

CHAPTER FIVE

Bradley decided he wasn't going to take the eye to work and show Charlie. It was an unnecessary risk, at least right now. He knew the cops had found the body. It'd been all over the local news. Bradley didn't return to Crystal's apartment since that would have been one of the dumbest things he could do. Many killers were caught when they returned to the scene of their crimes.

The eyeball rested in a plastic sandwich bag. Bradley had spent the last twenty-four hours thawing it. That was nothing to the time and investment he'd put into his garage. A drop in the bucket.

But everything would shortly be worth it. His garage. His temple. His place to find what was denied him. *No, don't you even think that!*

Bradley went to his garage, unlocked the door, and stepped inside. The cold immediately attacked him through the long-sleeve shirt and heavy jacket he wore. Over the past year, scrimping and saving, Bradley had turned his garage into a freezer—the entire thing. He'd put thermal lining across the walls, ceiling, and even the door.

He purchased two industrial air conditioners at five thousand dollars apiece. Mother was owed some thanks for that, of course. Mother *and* Father. God rest his soul.

The condensers pumped out air at fourteen degrees, twenty-four hours a day.

Bradley walked across the garage and stood at the center of the far wall. He carefully stuck his hand in his pocket and pulled out two tiny needles. He placed the eyeball against the wood at eye level, then, careful not to pierce the iris or pupil, he shoved the first needle through, and with a push, into the plywood beneath. The second needle followed the first.

Bradley took his hands away. Frost was already growing on the eye.

"There," he said. He stared at the single eyeball, seeing for the first time how it would look when he filled this entire room—every inch of the plywood—with eyes, all of them returning his stare.

He would have what he'd always wanted. What he'd always *deserved*.

Here. Does this smell like chloroform?

Bradley chuckled as he stared into his freezer later that night.

A woman lay unconscious in his living room, and Bradley had used that line just before he shoved the rag in her face. *Here. Does this smell like chloroform?* He thought it had been funny as hell. Couldn't stop laughing about it, actually.

He nodded as he stared at the empty garage—empty except for the eyeball at the back.

"I have to," he said, closing the door and returning to the living room.

The girl was unmarked. Bradley had done everything perfectly. One of Ted Bundy's quotes always stuck in his head, something like, *The first time you murder, you go through everything five hundred times to make sure it's perfect. The hundredth time you murder, you have to ask yourself where you put the tire iron.*

That wouldn't happen to Bradley.

And that was why he couldn't use the same methods every single time he killed. The Zodiac had known that, using different weapons and locations.

The first time, he had given the cops a hint about what he was doing, but he wouldn't do that again. One hint was enough for those bumbling idiots.

He didn't want to kill this girl in his house. That would create too much evidence, microscopic stuff he wasn't sure he could clean up.

The garage, though, could serve two purposes.

He grabbed the woman by the feet and pulled her across the living room and into the hallway.

"Hewwwooo?" she mumbled.

"Hewwo." Bradley smiled.

"Whah am I?" the girl asked.

"You're home now," he told her. The girl was waking, trying to slow herself down as he dragged her across the house. Her eyes were open and there was understanding behind them, if not the memory of what had happened.

"What is this?" she asked, her voice strengthening.

"Almost there," Bradley said, still smiling.

He turned the final corner and dragged her through the garage door. The girl tried to get up, so Bradley walked to her head and slammed his fist into the side of her face. She fell back to the floor, sobbing.

He pulled out a pair of handcuffs he'd bought at a novelty store on the seedy side of town. He slapped one on her wrist and one on the industrial machine pumping out all the cold air.

"See you in a little while," Bradley said. He walked out and closed the garage door behind him. It only took him a second to understand where he messed up. The girl's shrieks easily permeated the freezer. "Fuck." He had a room that was soundproof, but it wasn't the garage.

He went to the kitchen, gathered what he needed, and rushed back.

"That's not going to work for me," he said as he approached her with silver duct tape in one hand and a rag in the other. The woman tried to back up and get away from him, but there was nowhere to go.

"*PLEASE!*" she shrieked.

Bradley stopped walking toward her. "You want to go home?"

"Yes, please. *Please.* I won't tell."

"Tell you what. If you can survive a night in here and then me surgically removing your eyes, I'll let you go."

He crossed the distance, ignoring her shrieks, and

shoved the rag deep into her throat before wrapping the duct tape around her head.

Bradley wasn't tired when he got off work the next day. He had worked a twelve-hour shift, but it didn't feel it. He was like a kid at Christmas.

He drove home, following the speed limit, but only barely. He had told Charlie about what waited at the house, Charlie nodding along as usual. He was beginning to wonder if Charlie could actually understand the joy that came with what Bradley was doing. Perhaps no one could, not if they didn't experience it themselves.

Later, he told himself. *Now just get home.*

After he pulled into the driveway, he quickly made his way through the house, unlocked the garage door and stepped into his freezer.

"Oh, God!" A smile spread across his face in the room's cold darkness. "Oh, God, yes."

The girl sat against the industrial freezer, her head tilted down and to the left. Her eyes were open, and Bradley could see tiny ice crystals on her lashes. Her skin was blue with a white sheen; ice had formed on her.

Bradley walked over and knelt. He didn't try to lift her head, knowing the muscles and ligaments were frozen in place. Instead, he dipped his head so they stared into each other's eyes.

"Oh, yes. Yes. Yes."

The bright blue orbs were unharmed by the cold, ready to stare at him forever.

CHAPTER SIX

"I'm about to call it a night," Tommy said.

Christian didn't need to look at a clock to know the time. It was well past three in the morning. The paperwork was finished, and they knew what they would say to the rest of the police and agents tomorrow. Well, actually, today, at seven in the morning.

Christian hadn't been alone much in the last thirty-six hours, and he could barely stand it. He had managed to keep from saying it out loud, though.

"Sounds good," Luke said from the whiteboard. He hadn't written anything on it, only stared at it for the past thirty minutes.

"He does that," Tommy had said. "You just have to get used to it."

"Christian," Luke called from across the room. "I can give you a ride home if you'd like?"

"I'd rather call a taxi," he blurted out, unable to hold it back.

Luke and Tommy both laughed.

"Well, you might rather, but that's not happening," Luke said, stepping back from the whiteboard and walking to one of the chairs at the bar. He pulled his jacket off it. "Let's go. You're only a half hour from here."

The three walked upstairs and onto the grounds of Luke's estate.

"How much money do you have?" Christian asked. "Like, just a general amount is fine. I don't need it down to the pennies."

Tommy shook his head and unlocked his car door. "I'll see you two in a few hours. Try to get some sleep."

The door closed, and Christian looked at Luke. The driveway they stood on was a quarter of a mile long from house to gate. It ended in a circle in front of the house with a small garden in the middle. Lights illuminated the front of the house, casting artful shadows while showing off the superb landscaping.

"I don't have a lot of taste," Christian said, "but all this looks really nice. I imagine it's pretty expensive to keep up. How much are you worth?"

"Somewhere between three and five million," Luke replied. "Let's go."

Christian climbed into the car, which was easily the most expensive one he'd ever sat in. It was electric, and when Luke started it, no sound emanated from the engine.

"That's weird," Christian said, though he had known it would happen. "I'm used to hearing the engine crank up."

"You get used to this, too," Luke assured him.

Christian looked at Luke as they circled the driveway. His hair was short and wavy, his face thin and angular. The shirt he wore wasn't tight, but Christian could see muscle beneath.

"I wanted to talk to you, Christian," he began.

"About what?"

"What you did today. How did you know what was in the eye? Tommy wasn't paying attention, and neither was Roger, so both of them thought you looked up to see it. You didn't, though. You knew what was there before it'd been pulled out."

Christian turned his head and stared out the window.

"I don't know."

"I think you do. I'd like you to tell me."

"I just... I'm starting to see him. I can't explain it any better than that." Christian hated talking about this. He had hated it in grade school when his teachers asked him how he knew who stole something from their desk. He'd hated it in college when he was able to make massive jumps of logic that none of the other students could. He hated explaining himself.

"Don't go away, Christian. Don't go into yourself. I saw you do that for a short time today. I'd like you to speak to me now. What do you mean, you're starting to see him?"

Christian sighed. "I, uh... Do you have a girlfriend?"

"Me? Not for some time," Luke said.

"Have you had one?"

"Yes, in the past."

"I've never had one, so this might not be right, but I imagine the more time you spend around a woman, the more you can anticipate her thoughts and actions. Things like that. Am I right?"

"Yes."

"Well, the more time I spend around the crime scene, the more clearly I can see him. The major difference is that I see his past. I understand what made him do this."

Luke didn't look over and was quiet for a second before saying, "You think his past will help us find him?"

"Numbers follow the logic inherent within them. Humans follow the logic inside them as well, only that logic was built off their past. If we understand someone's past, we'll understand their future."

Luke drove back to his house alone. He kept the windows rolled up and the radio off, listening to the sound of the car's tires rotating at a hundred miles an hour down the highway.

Luke had waited two years without beginning what he came here to do. Partly, that was because he needed to increase his bona fides and partly because he wanted to learn the landscape. Now he'd accomplished both goals and had seriously been considering starting.

He didn't know what to do with Christian Windsor, though.

The kid was emotionally stunted but had abilities the rest of the world could barely imagine. Even with his arrested emotional development, Christian understood his gifts well. The comparison to a girlfriend had been masterful.

Luke switched lanes, passing a car without looking at it.

Luke didn't worry. He never did. The world had been easy since his earliest memories from the age of two. There was nothing to worry about once you understood that even God couldn't strike you down.

Ten years ago, he'd decided why he had been placed here. He had played around with his purpose in academia, but he'd realized he would reach his full potential within the FBI.

He didn't fear Christian Windsor but thought the boy could make things harder for him. His intelligence rivaled Luke's, and his insight into human behavior... Luke had worked to mask his past so the truth of his birth and adolescence would never be known by anyone, but if Christian could understand his past simply by being around him...

Luke would need to deal with that.

Christian walked up the stairs to his condo. He'd kept it while he was at Quantico, renting it out until this last semester when he knew he might return. It looked nothing like Luke's house, but that was okay with Christian. He didn't think he'd be able to handle something that large, especially not living by himself. He liked the smallness of his condominium. It reminded him of his mom's house.

He put his bag down on the kitchen table and picked up the landline.

"Hello?"

"Hey, Mom. Sorry to wake you. I just wanted to let you know I'm home."

"I wasn't asleep. You know I haven't been sleeping well lately."

"I know. Did you take melatonin?"

"No. We both know it doesn't work, and you're just trying to use it as a placebo on me," she said.

Christian smiled. He rarely did so around other people, but his mother brought it out.

"Get some sleep, son. Call me tomorrow, okay?"

"Okay, Mom."

Christian hung up, then pulled his computer out of his bag and walked to his bedroom. He laid down and opened the laptop on his chest, then started his music program. He placed the computer at his side and let the songs run through their endless loop.

He'd been able to explain what he did to Luke because he'd had to do it before. People had been asking him that question his entire life—how he did what he did. His mother had helped him figure out the answer about the girlfriend. Christian wouldn't have thought of that in a million years.

His eyes glazed over, and he found himself in the room named Surgeon.

The music playing in his bedroom couldn't make its way in here. He was alone, his mind his only company.

"What happened to you?" he asked as he stared at the pictures on the wall. The headless torso, the cut ragged and rough. Whoever had done this wasn't used to cutting things, not yet. "Maybe you don't like it. Maybe you only did that to convey the message that you're brutal."

It had been unnecessary to cut the head off when what he apparently wanted were the eyes, or one of them.

Christian looked to his right and saw the room moving, remodeling itself to fit his needs. The digital wall turned into a door. He went to it, knowing that by the time he crossed the threshold, the rest would be ready on the other side.

He opened it and found himself in a dark room. He heard the door close behind him, but there was no fear in this place, regardless of how black it was. Christian feared the outside world, but his mind ruled here.

Christian Windsor finds himself in someone else's life. The room he just stood in is gone, just as reality left when he entered his mansion.

Now he stands in someone else's home, though much of it is hazy. This happens when he's first learning about someone. He can't see everything correctly in the beginning because he doesn't know the person well enough yet.

The house isn't small, like Christian's apartment. He walks through the living room, the furniture looking like smudged ink, unable to make out much more than the shape of chairs or couches. He heads to a bedroom, and finally, the room clears up some.

He sees a single bed against the wall and a small television sitting on a chest of drawers. A computer is on a table.

"You're not married," he says to the empty room. "No one ever comes over to your place, though it's big enough to have them if you wanted. You're lonely, though you don't know it. You've been lonely your whole life, haven't you?"

This strengthens Christian's vision, the connection between him and this killer. Loneliness. Christian understood loneliness even if the man who lived here couldn't. He moves to the drawers but doesn't pull them open. He knows that he will see nothing but a hazy dream world if he does since his vision is not strong enough for that yet.

He looks to his left and sees an open bathroom door. Through it, he sees a clean sink. A single toothbrush sits in a holder, yet he sees no toothpaste. No discarded medicine bottles. No hair.

"You're clean. Meticulous, even. You think that's going to help you do all of this because you won't leave anything for anyone to find."

Christian waits for a second, staring at the bathroom though not venturing into it. "It might not be your first, but it's close to it." The thought comes to him in a giant leap. The bathroom gives it to him. Its cleanliness. Murder affects people's minds, and this person's mind hasn't been changed yet. It hasn't been *altered*.

"It's not going to be your last, is it?"

Later that morning, Tommy stood in front of a room full of police officers. Luke was to his right and Christian sat in the back left of the room, as close to the corner as he could get without melting into it.

"Okay," Tommy began. "As far as evidence, we have a partial shoeprint from the left shoe, made with blood. No fingerprints. We have nothing under the victim's nails and no wounds on the victim's body—"

"Outside of the head being chopped off?" someone asked from within the crowd.

"Yes, besides that. No other bruises. The autopsy revealed chloroform residue in the lungs, which we suspect was how the killer kept her from fighting him. He murdered her right after applying the chloroform, which means he cut her head off while she was still alive." Tommy took a sip from the water glass on the small podium. "The victim's eyes were removed, completely."

"They're calling him the Surgeon. How neat was the cut?" someone asked.

Luke cleared his throat, and Tommy looked at him since he could speak to medical questions better.

"The cut on the neck wasn't neat. He basically hacked at it until the head separated from the body. The eyes were different. Care was taken, and the cuts were nearly surgical in their precision. He excavated the eyes in a way that kept them from being damaged. Even when he placed the eye in the victim's mouth, it was intact."

"What was found inside?" another cop asked.

"The eye?"

"Yes."

"A sliver of someone else's eye, but not this victim's," Luke explained. "The eye colors were different shades, but we ran DNA tests to ensure the victim didn't have two different color irises. There was no match."

"So, this wasn't his first victim?"

"We don't believe so, no," Tommy replied.

"It's the first victim he doesn't personally know." Christian's voice was abnormally loud as if he wasn't sure anyone could hear him if he lowered it. Tommy glanced at the corner of the room, but Christian wasn't looking up. He leaned forward, elbows on his knees, and stared at the floor. "The sliver of eye came from someone he knew. It might be someone who's already dead. This, in the killer's mind, is the first person he's done this to."

In their talks, Christian hadn't said anything about that, although in his favor, the question hadn't come up. Tommy had figured the answer was no, given that someone else's eye was found *inside* their victim.

He wouldn't contradict Christian right now, though. "This is Agent Christian Windsor. He's working with us on this case. I don't want it going out that there is disagreement between the three of us. If Christian says this is the first murder, then it is. Does anyone have any other questions?"

CHAPTER SEVEN

"Thawing the body took a long time," Bradley said. "Much longer than I thought it would. I don't know if I'll do that again."

Charles and Bradley were outside on the lawn. Bradley had said Charles wanted to get outdoors for a few minutes, though Charles had wanted no such thing. The bastard was using it as an excuse to talk more. Always talking.

Charles now knew Bradley wasn't lying. He had seen the news this morning. A body had been found decapitated, just as Bradley had said.

"They didn't tell everything, though. They never do." He was standing behind Charles' wheelchair. "I won't go into details of what they left out in case you get the wise idea of telling someone about our conversations, but the police keep things from the public. This way, they can tell the difference between crackpots and actual leads."

Goddammit, Charles thought. *God-fucking-dammit.*

The bastard thought of everything. Any piece of information Charles might be able to use against him was withheld.

"Are your children coming to visit you soon, Charlie? I looked at the guest register, and it's been a month since anyone's been here. Go ahead. Write out your answer."

Charles reached into the bag at his side and pulled out the tablet the nursing home supplied him with—supposedly one of the great amenities. He turned it on and loaded the word processing "app," as they now called these things. They used to be called programs. The whole damn world was insane, changing names needlessly and cutting off people's heads.

He used the digital pen to scribble on the tablet.

Two weeks, I think.

"Why don't they come more often?"

Vacation. Europe.

"Ah," Bradley said. "I didn't go too far back in the records. Do they usually come regularly?"

Every two weeks.

"That's good. Do you miss them?"

Charles paused. What did he want to tell this man? And could he lie? Would the bastard know if he did?

Yes, he wrote.

"Well, when they come, Charlie, you know better than to speak about this, right?"

Yes.

"Good. I thought so. I just wanted to check. We should probably head back in. I've got to make my rounds."

Relief flooded Charles. The bastard's rounds were to Charles what water was to a desert plant.

They moved through the nursing home's back door and into the common area.

"I'll catch up with you later, Charlie," Bradley said, giving a little wave as he walked away.

I've got to do something, Charles thought. *I can't keep going through this.*

"That's awful," one of the old hags sitting in the room said. Charles looked at the television. A police press conference about the decapitation was on the screen.

Bradley didn't do his rounds. He would get to them when he had time, and right now, he didn't. The police were holding a press conference, and he needed to hear what they had to say. The news kept things from the public during their reporting, but maybe the cops would give out more information.

He entered the employee break room, fully expecting some cow to have it on a talk show. Bradley had a plan to get them to change it, nothing too obnoxious. He knew better than to make a scene.

Luckily, the television was on the press conference. The other two people in the room were sitting down and staring at the screen in the corner.

"How long's this been on?" Bradley asked.

"Just a few minutes," Cheryl replied.

"Is there any truth to the rumor that something was removed from the victim's body?" a reporter asked.

"I can't comment on that. What I will say is any evidence we've found is being looked at carefully and diligently."

So, someone had leaked about the eyes. Maybe Crystal's family. Maybe someone in the police department.

"Sir, why is the FBI involved in this case?"

Bradley's mouth opened slightly, just enough that his lips no longer touched. The FBI? For one murder? He'd figured they would get involved, but he'd thought it would take time. Perhaps he could fill much of his garage before then.

"We're here supporting the police force, but due to the ruthless nature of the crime, we feel it's best to be involved early," the agent said.

"Do you think this might be a serial killer?" a reporter asked.

"There's no evidence to support that at the current time."

Bradley looked at the other two people in the room. Neither returned his glance. "Psycho, huh?"

"Yeah, pretty bad," an older black orderly said. Bradley thought his name was Reggie but couldn't remember.

"Back to work," Bradley said, turning from the room and walking into the hallway. He didn't stop walking once outside the break room but kept going, his mind on autopilot, taking him through the rounds he needed to complete. His conscious mind focused on the damned FBI. They shouldn't be here this early. The FBI got involved when things crossed state lines, and only then if the murders could be connected to one another. Yet, here they were, right there on the goddamn television screen.

The ruthless nature.

Was that how they saw him? Saw what he did? They didn't know what the fuck a *ruthless nature* was. If the FBI wanted to see it, Bradley would show them. He'd put on a fucking clinic like his father had for him.

CHAPTER EIGHT

Luke Titan wasn't what Veronica Lopez had expected. She, of course, had seen dozens of pictures and had even watched some of the speeches he had given, but somehow, she'd thought he'd be nerdier.

The man in front of her had no visible qualities she associated with a nerd, however.

"So, Ms. Lopez, do you realize the awkwardness of what you're doing yet?"

This was their first meeting. Everything had been arranged by Veronica's publicist, ensuring that Titan would work with her throughout the project.

"What's that?" she asked, smiling. She wondered if Titan would take this seriously. She'd heard that he only took his *own* projects seriously, and everything else was beneath him.

"You're writing a book on work that hasn't been finished yet. We aren't sure that what we designed will do what we expect."

"You left the project, though, right? You wouldn't have

done that if you didn't think it would succeed," Veronica countered.

Titan shrugged. "I left it in good hands. I just think it might be premature to write an entire book on the Sphere."

"Well, I think the market will disagree. This is going to be a huge best seller."

"How many of the other scientists are working with you?" Titan asked.

"All of them."

"Bridgette?"

Veronica nodded. "Yes, she's contributing."

"Good. She's a smart one. Where would you like to begin?"

Veronica pulled her cellphone out of her purse and placed it on the coffee table. "I'll be recording all of this. That's okay, right?"

"Of course."

"Great. Thanks." She tapped the screen a few times, and then they were ready to go. "Tell me in your own words what the Sphere is meant to do. I think that's as good a place to start as any."

Veronica's mind was simultaneously ablaze and exhausted.

She looked at her cellphone with dread. She had to play the recording, and if she did that right now, she wouldn't sleep for the rest of the night. She would stay up listening to Titan's words, trying to parse them and understand what he said on a deeper level than she had the first time.

Because the man was brilliant.

Beyond brilliant. Easily the smartest person working on the project.

There had been rumors that when he left, the Sphere's forward movement to a market-ready endeavor had slowed considerably. The other scientists Veronica had interviewed had denied it, but now she knew the truth. The Sphere might still make it to market—it *had* to, with all the money the government had sunk into it—but when Titan had left, a large part of the brainpower behind it had left with him.

Veronica ignored the phone and turned to the kitchen. She went to the refrigerator and grabbed a bottle of cheap white wine. She poured herself a glass, then left the bottle on the counter and sipped the wine.

People working on the project called it the Sphere. The actual name was Orbital Monitoring System, and the idea had been Luke Titan's. It was a joint effort between the private and public sectors, with everyone from governments to research universities giving up prominent scientists to join the project. A major reason for getting on board was the prestige that came with it.

When she'd asked Titan to describe the Sphere, his answer had been the simplest and the most accurate so far.

"It's humanity's best chance to continue living on Earth."

Veronica had countered, "What about the argument that we should be worrying about the human impact of living *on* Earth? Global warming and such?"

"Legitimate question, but I'll leave that for someone else to figure out. I wanted to make sure that nothing from *outside* destroys us."

The problem, as Luke Titan had seen it, was that virtually no one was looking toward the sky. In fact, when he first introduced the idea of the Sphere, you could fit everyone looking for asteroids, across the entire world, inside two McDonald's restaurants. Asteroids passed by Earth all the time, and it only took missing one—the sky watchers missed about eighty-five percent, though most moved by without hitting Earth's atmosphere—and the entire human population would be wiped out.

"These types of extinction events can't be predicted with any regularity, but they do happen. The last major one landed in the American Midwest."

The Sphere would take care of any asteroids that could harm Earth. It would circle the planet like a satellite but monitor a gazillion light years outward, ensuring that any asteroids would be seen long before they had a chance to crash into Earth.

Then Luke Titan left the project. He had quit and joined the FBI, of all things. Veronica hadn't asked him about that, but she was at least as curious about his change of direction as anything else. It made no sense, not to anyone that used to work with him on the Sphere and certainly not to her.

"Not tonight," she said and stepped away from the phone. She went into her living room and sat down, turning on the television. There'd be plenty of time to think about Luke Titan.

CHAPTER NINE

At two in the morning, Christian finally came across something useful. He'd been on his computer for the past three hours, having spent the rest of the day sitting in on interviews with Tommy and Luke. He didn't speak much in them, only took in the information Crystal Hembree's parents and coworkers gave. Nothing he heard granted him a clearer picture of the man they were hunting, though.

Crystal hadn't known the killer, or at least, what she did know about him wasn't true. None of her family or friends would have known him either.

The eye removal made Christian think the man would move in quick succession. He was a collector, obviously, but the eyes meant something very intimate. They were called the windows of the soul. People averted their eyes when lying. Christian himself could barely stand to look at someone else's.

The eyes.

The hacking of the head, the eye in the mouth, all of

that had been for show. The only thing that mattered was the eye he took and the sliver he'd left inside the other eyeball... Christian wasn't ready to venture down that road yet, though.

The eyes. The killer would want more of them, and soon. Whatever he was doing with them, whatever purpose they served, one wasn't enough. But he couldn't leave the bodies of each person he took for others to find, not if he wanted to stay out of custody. He had to know that.

Christian had started pulling missing person reports for the five counties surrounding the one where Crystal Hembree turned up.

The past week there had been two missing persons, one of whom had been found and one who seemed to be a runaway.

Tonight, a family had reported someone new.

The police required two days before someone could be classified as missing, which meant this person had been gone for at least forty-eight hours.

Christian pulled up the picture. Another woman, age twenty-five. Blonde hair. Pretty but not beautiful. White. Christian zeroed in on her eyes.

Blue.

Just like Crystal Hembree's.

They weren't as dynamic but more subtle. Gentler, maybe.

Christian stared at the woman's eyes for an hour or more.

A little before dawn, he closed his computer and rolled over on his side. He looked at the nightstand next to him, wondering if this was a route he should venture down.

Before, when he'd used what his mother called his gift, it had been for innocent things. If not innocent, certainly not evil. Could he do this without losing himself?

The appointment had been scheduled for six in the morning. Melissa didn't do this for other patients, but she understood that Christian Windsor wasn't like anyone else. All of them had special needs and were individuals. They all had to be treated differently, but Christian was special even among them. Now that he was back in Atlanta, she'd have to make accommodations for him.

She stepped into her waiting area, a coffee mug in her hand.

"Ready?" she asked.

"I'm sorry. I know you don't like working these hours," Christian greeted her.

"It's fine. I'm normally in the office anyway, just not seeing patients yet. Come on back."

She let him lead the way to her office, a path they both knew by heart. Christian had no problem taking the lead in here, which meant he felt safe. He felt this was as much his home as hers. It had taken him two years to do that. He'd always let her lead, following a foot or two behind, then one day, he'd taken over without saying anything.

He sat on the leather couch, and she moved to the leather chair to the left of it. He hadn't been in this office in quite a while, but he still sat in the same corner of the couch. Some people sat in the middle, and yes, even that said something about the person. Those in the corner said they weren't sure what the world would throw at them. Those in the middle said it didn't matter what came. They would handle it.

"Where would you like to start?" she asked.

Christian stared at the picture on the other wall, as he always did when they spoke in here.

"I'm not going to be able to do this job."

"You took it?"

He nodded.

"It's a bit early to decide you can't do it, isn't it? When people first take a job, they often feel they're in too deep. That it's too much for them."

"You don't understand," he said.

"Then help me to do so."

"What I do, what I'm able to do, I don't like it. I never have. But I'm not able to stop it. It's why I wanted to be an analyst in the first place. I can use this thing with numbers the same way I can with people. The numbers aren't going to take me into dark places. This will. I don't know if I'm strong enough to go there."

"What kinds of dark places?"

"I'm not sure I can talk to you about an open case."

"You can. I'm legally and morally obliged to keep this private from everyone unless you give me permission to do otherwise. Everything we discuss will remain confidential as long as you're not going to harm yourself or someone else."

Christian was quiet for a few moments.

"I stared at a woman's eyes for a long time last night. Her eyes were beautiful."

"Were?" Melissa asked. "Is she dead?"

"Most likely. She's a missing person."

"You think the man you're chasing took her?"

He nodded. "When I stared at her eyes, I saw more about him."

"How?"

"I don't know. I've never known how. In college, the more I listened to a professor speak, the more I knew about their past. In economics, I wrote a paper that was published by *The Quarterly Journal of Economics* at the Oxford Press." He didn't look at her with the last sentence. Didn't show any pride about that happening to someone so young.

Melissa knew he was likely the first undergraduate to be published there. "The paper linked the professors' pasts to the schools of economics they chose. I ran linear regressions after I understood the childhoods of a few of my professors and found striking correlations that could link people to free markets or centralized markets. I don't know how I did that any more than I know how I'm doing this."

"What's the problem, then?" she asked.

"The problem is that this man's past wasn't healthy. I don't want to see what dwells in it, and I'm not sure how it's going to affect me. I'm getting close to not being able to pull back, though. I'm going to want to see this to the end, just like I do everything else."

"You can always pull back, Christian. It's just more difficult for you," Melissa reminded him. His autism, as they both knew, created a severe desire to finish things he started and a focus that resembled a bullet—once the path was set, he didn't deviate if he could help it. Still, he *could* pull back if he tried.

"No, Melissa." Christian shook his head. "I can't, and you know it." He finally turned away from the picture and looked at her. "Do you think it will mess my mind up if I keep following this guy?"

Melissa was quiet for a few moments, unsure of how to answer. She knew what she said next would have a profound impact. It could even determine whether he quit his job. Further, she couldn't dismiss the possibility that he simply didn't want to do this job. That he was putting up a defense to try to avoid doing something meaningful.

"I don't know," she finally said honestly. "I can't say for sure until you've worked a bit longer. I will promise you that if I think it's affecting you negatively, I'll tell you and ask you to stop."

"That's what you don't understand, Melissa," Christian replied. "Once I really start, no one will be able to stop me. In that way, this guy and I are a lot alike."

Luke looked at Tommy. His partner was enraptured by the boy, listening to his words the way a dog listens to someone holding a morsel of food. Luke wasn't jealous of the way Tommy lapped up Christian's words, only intensely interested.

Christian didn't understand the effect he had on people. He had no idea that when he spoke, he could make people stop in their tracks and listen simply due to his intelligence.

It was a power that could be used if the wielder under-stood what they were doing.

"Well, we need to call in the parents," Tommy said. "Right away. Luke, what do you think?"

"Good detective work, Christian. I'm curious why you think he's targeting people with blue eyes?"

The boy stared at Luke's desk. The group had gathered in his office this morning. "I don't know. It's clearly some-thing to do with both the eyes and the color, but I'm not sure how they correlate yet."

"Do you think you'll figure that out?" Luke asked, a slight smirk on his face. "Or will that be beyond you?" If Christian heard the sarcasm, it wasn't apparent.

"I'll figure it out," he said. The room fell silent.

"All right," Tommy finally said. "Christian, can you get the parents' numbers? I'll call them."

"I already have them. Do you want them now?"

Tommy laughed. Luke kept his smirk planted on his face.

"Give me a minute with Luke, okay? Nothing impor-tant. Just want to ask him something in private."

"Sure." Christian walked out of the room.

Tommy turned in his chair and looked at Luke across the desk. "What the hell was that?"

"What?"

"What you just asked the kid. Whether he would be able to figure it out?"

Luke leaned back. He was enjoying this, though it didn't show on his face. Tommy was taking a paternal stance over the boy, and that could play a role in what came next. "We joke with each other, don't we? Do you think we shouldn't include him in jokes because he's a bit different?"

"A *bit* different, Luke? The kid is two breaths away from being seriously disabled. He's a genius, no doubt, but 'different' isn't how I'd describe him."

"I think you're underestimating him. He's nowhere near handicapped, just not comfortable enough around us to open up. By joking with him, we can probably help him."

"If he understands that we're joking," Tommy said.

"He will."

"All right. I'm not going to argue about this. Just take it easy on him, okay? For me, if not for the kid's sake."

"Sure," Luke said.

"I'm going to go call the parents. Let's try to talk to them today. You want to do it, or do you want me to?"

Luke looked outside his office. The boy was standing at his desk, having not sat down yet. "I'll do it. I'll bring Windsor with me."

"Mr. and Mrs. York, I'm Special Agent Luke Titan. This is Agent Christian Windsor. You spoke to our partner over the phone. We will be conducting today's interview."

The two sat in a simple interview room. One wall had a two-way mirror, and a table rested in the middle of the room. Christian and Luke sat on one side, and the obviously frightened parents sat on the other.

"You're Luke Titan?" Mr. York asked. "*The* Luke Titan?"

"Yes, but my reputation's been greatly overblown. Right now, I'm only concerned about finding your daughter

Lauren. Same with Christian here. We need to start by discussing the last time you heard from or saw Lauren."

"We already explained all this to the police, but they were too concerned with that freak show you guys held the news conference about. She's not involved in that, right? You're not talking to us because she might be a part of what that psycho is up to, are you?"

"We need to know her last known location. Once we have that, we'll be in a much better place to find her." Luke's voice was calm and collected despite the increasing panic in the father's voice.

"I talked to her three days ago," Mrs. York said. "We spoke about what she wanted me to cook for her birthday dinner this Sunday. She said she was going out with her friends on Saturday, but Sunday, she'd be over for dinner. She turned twenty-three yesterday." Tears swam in the woman's eyes, but she fought to keep them from falling.

"And you called her the next day?"

"No," Mrs. York replied. "She normally calls me every day, or if not every day, four or five times a week. I usually wait for her."

"When did you finally call?" Luke asked.

"Sunday morning. I was surprised when I hadn't heard from her because of the dinner I was cooking."

"No answer, though, correct? Did you call her friends?"

Mrs. York nodded, and her voice cracked as she spoke. "They didn't hear from her on Saturday. They said they had all planned to go out, but she didn't answer her phone all day."

"Thank you, Mrs. York. We'll need their names and

numbers before you leave so we can talk with them as well. Does Lauren have a boyfriend?"

"She did," Mr. York said. "She stopped dating him six months ago. His name is Tucker Heraldson. We'll get you his number."

"Agent Windsor," Luke said, turning to his left. "Do you have any questions you'd like to ask?" Luke didn't care what the parents had to say. He knew their daughter was dead and her eyes had been removed. They would know it soon, too. What Luke really wanted to see was how the boy acted in interviews, how his mind worked, and what he would try to find out.

"Mr. and Mrs. York," Christian began, and Luke saw the effort it took for him to raise his eyes to meet theirs. "Do you have the passwords for any social networks your daughter used?"

"Umm, I don't believe so," the mother said.

"We can probably get them, though," Mr. York followed up. "Can we give them to you later today?"

"Yes." Christian looked back down.

"If you don't mind me asking, why are they important?"

Luke didn't look at Christian as he spoke, already knowing the answer. "It would have been the easiest way for her abductor to make contact."

And to see her eyes, Luke thought.

CHAPTER TEN

"You think he made contact online?"

Christian, Tommy, and Luke sat in Luke's office again. The day was nearly over, or rather, the day was over for everyone else. The three of them were the only ones left.

Christian stared out the window, tired. "Yes."

"Why?" Luke asked.

"You already know," Christian said. "Why do you ask me questions you know the answers to?" He didn't glance at Luke but saw the looks his partners gave each other.

"I just want to hear your answers."

"It's easier to meet these people online than in person. In person creates too many ways for him to get caught. Her friends meeting him. Him being seen with her. The internet provides anonymity."

"Yeah, but it leaves a trail, too," Tommy countered. "Everything you do online is categorized and saved."

"True," Christian said, "but if our guy is clever, which I'm beginning to think he is, there are ways to mask your identity. I bet when we get the passwords, someone new will have contacted her. His profile and digital thumbprint will be a lie, but he'll be the one we want."

Three eyeballs stared at Bradley. He wore a heavy coat, a scarf, and a skullcap. He'd been standing in the freezer for a while, though he had lost track of time. He couldn't say how many hours. His cheeks were red and his hands were numb despite keeping them in his pockets. He didn't care.

He couldn't pull himself away from the eyes. He didn't like that he only had three. It should have been an even number. Each eye should have a partner. The first didn't, though, because he had wanted to leave a message for the goddamn cops.

Should he throw it out?

"No," Bradley said. "No, that was too much work. Keep it. Maybe move it to the corner."

He nodded. Yes, that would work. He'd move it away from these two.

He pulled the two needles out and held the organic ice cube in his hand. He walked across the garage, knelt on the floor, and pinned the eyeball down low.

"There." He nodded again. "That's better."

Finally, Bradley left the garage. He closed the door, locking the deadbolt behind him. He looked at the door for a second and wondered if he should install a padlock. He didn't think Mother could get to it, but you never knew. That was one of the reasons Dahmer had been caught; he'd been careless. He'd kept a vat of bodies *inside his apartment.*

Right there in the open, the smell of decomposing flesh filling his kitchen and living room.

Well, you do have a room with frozen eyeballs.

Which was why he needed the padlock. The more security, the better.

Bradley took his skullcap off and went down the hall. He walked through the house, pulling the scarf from his neck. He took his jacket off as he reached Mother's room.

He knocked on the door.

"What?" she called from inside.

"Are you hungry? I have to go to work soon, so I wanted to make sure you eat before I go."

"I'm not hungry," Mother replied.

Bradley turned from the door and went to the kitchen. He pulled bread, mayonnaise, and sliced turkey out of the refrigerator. It took him a few minutes because his hands were so cold, but he made a sandwich and put it on a plate. Bradley brought it back to her room and set it in front of her door.

"Mother, there's a sandwich here if you get hungry. I'll be back this evening."

"Why are you spending so much time in the garage?" she asked.

Bradley swallowed, and his left hand started shaking. He didn't notice either of the movements.

"I'm remodeling it," he explained.

"Why?"

"I want it to look nice."

A pause.

"Are you doing something you shouldn't?"

Again, Bradley swallowed, unable to help himself. "No."

He stood, waiting to see if she would continue pestering him. Mother said nothing, though, and finally, Bradley left the house. His left hand was still shaking, and his mind was blank with fury.

She was *always* pestering him.

Charles Ranger had spent the last twenty-four hours making up his mind. He couldn't continue living like this. It was bad enough that he couldn't speak, but having to listen to that psychopath continually talking was unbearable. He couldn't go on like this.

His children were coming to visit him today, and he'd decided to tell them everything, or rather, to write it all down and let them read it. He spent the last few hours of the night scribbling the truth on his tablet.

At six in the morning, he finally fell asleep, making sure to turn the tablet off and put it away before he did. Opening his eyes to Bradley looking down at his note wouldn't be in Charles' best interests; that was certain.

"Wake up, sleepyhead."

Charles heard the voice, but it felt far away.

Something grabbed his shoulder roughly, and that *wasn't* far away. His eyes flashed open, and Bradley stood above him.

"You overslept," the psychopath said.

Charles blinked a few times as his mind tried to catch up with his surroundings.

"Your kids will be here in an hour. You need to get ready."

Bradley didn't look well, and that was saying something because the psycho never looked great. Today, though, was different. Had he been crying? His eyes were red and puffy.

Something's wrong, Charles thought. Does he know? Did he see my tablet?

Charles managed to keep himself from glancing at his nightstand, where he kept the digital device. He could see it peripherally, though, and the drawer wasn't open. If Bradley had seen what he wrote, he'd put it away again.

Don't be a damned fool. The psychopath wasn't crying because you wrote a note to your kids, telling them what he's doing. If he read it, you'd already be dead.

"I haven't had a good morning," Bradley said.

He sounds like a robot, Charles thought. As if he's never felt an emotion in his entire life.

Charles knew that wasn't true, though. He'd heard Bradley get really animated when he discussed his little eyeball project.

Bradley didn't look down as he continued speaking. He stared at Charles' headboard. "I know your kids are coming today, and if you tell them what I've been telling you, I'll kill them. I've seen them, and their eyes aren't that pretty, so they won't make it on my wall. You know what I've been doing with the last body, Charlie? I'm eating it. I'm feeding it to Mother, too.

"You see, if there's no body, there's no crime. I'm making broth with the bones. There's a lot of healthy stuff in bone broth, collagen and stuff like that. I'll eat your kids, Charlie, if you tell them, and I promise, it's not like those Hannibal Lecter books. It's a brutal effort to cut up a body, getting through gristle and bone." Bradley looked down, his eyes clearing as if he'd realized he'd been speaking aloud. "You don't want that to happen, do you?"

Charles shook his head. He believed this madman. To tell his children would be to kill them.

Maybe Bradley had gone too far with Charlie this morning. He wasn't sure and truly couldn't remember everything he'd said. When Mother made him mad, he lost himself in his thoughts for some time after. That was why he had punished her, though it wasn't as bad as Father's punishments. Didn't she see that? Bradley couldn't afford to get lost right now. If he did, he'd get caught. When Bradley had decided to start his wall, it was under the assumption that he'd never be caught.

He wouldn't end up like Dahmer, stabbed to death in jail.

Dahmer had been an idiot, though. He'd only gone on for so long because the cops were even dumber. Bradley was no idiot.

Bradley kept an eye on Charlie while his kids visited, though he couldn't watch the old man as closely as he wanted to. He still had work to do. From what he saw, though, nothing out of the ordinary came up. Charlie might have been a bit downtrodden, but that probably had to do with what Bradley had said. He'd speak to Charlie about it tomorrow. The man needed to know he had to keep his mouth shut, and as long as he did that, he had nothing to worry about. Not yet.

Bradley went through the rest of the day with as much

gusto as a slug crossing hot asphalt. He hated being here because he had things to do at home, teaching Mother a lesson being not the least of them. Finally, though, the day ended, and he found himself standing outside Mother's bedroom door.

The sandwich hadn't been touched.

"Why didn't you eat?" he said, without bothering to knock or announce himself.

"I told you I wasn't hungry."

"What you said this morning, Mother? That wasn't polite." His voice shook, as did his left hand. He heard his voice and hated it. He sounded weak.

"What are you doing in that garage, Bradley?" she asked.

"It's none of your goddamn business, Mother."

"This is still my house. Everything that goes on inside it is my business."

Bradley opened the bedroom door and crossed the threshold from the hallway to the room. The smell came first, as it always did. The room smelled dead, like the inside of a coffin, all stale air and long-decayed flesh.

The room was dark, the only light coming from a lamp in the back corner of the room.

Mother lay in her bed. The television was turned off.

"What do you want?" she asked. "I didn't say you could come in."

Bradley walked across the room and stood next to the bed. She didn't turn her head to look at him.

"I've told you not to talk to me like that. I'm not a child anymore."

"No, you're definitely not a child." Her voice was

subdued, and Bradley enjoyed *that*. It meant she was learning. She knew who was in charge, even if she didn't want it to be so.

"You're going to respect me, Mother. Father is gone, and he's not coming back. You're going to respect me, or I'll teach you to. You understand?"

Mother turned her head toward the window but said nothing.

Bradley looked at her frail body. She needed to eat. "You're not going on a hunger strike. If I have to force-feed you, I will."

"I'll eat when I'm hungry."

Bradley felt the blood rise to his face again, anger wanting to overflow onto Mother and her goddamn bed. Her thin legs stuck out, the lamp's light making the scars rise almost incandescently from her skin. They had healed, but they wouldn't always. One day, the cuts would be too much for her old body to handle, and she'd die.

"You should be careful, Mother," Bradley cautioned. "You're not as young as you used to be."

He stared at her for a minute or so, though she didn't look at him. Maybe she didn't know he was looking at her. She kept silent, though, and that was most important.

Bradley left the room, closing the door behind him. He looked down at the sandwich. The meat was gray now.

A waste of good meat.

He kicked it across the hall, and the bread flew off. The thick piece of meat hit the wall with a splat.

Bradley watched it fall before walking down the hallway to his room.

CHAPTER ELEVEN

"That's him," Christian said.

"You're sure?" Tommy asked from behind him. Luke stood to Tommy's right. Christian sat in the chair, staring at the laptop.

"Yes. He's the one we want."

Tommy looked at the picture on the screen. The guy was good-looking. Young, at least compared to Tommy. More and more, he felt everyone was young compared to him. Forty-five wasn't as glamorous as he wanted it to be. The man was probably in his mid-twenties, which fit the profile.

"That's not *actually* him, though, right?" Tommy asked.

"No. It's a fake photo." Christian looked at Tommy, no shyness on his face for once. Instead, Tommy saw intense concentration.

This is the real him, Tommy thought. This is the part of him that feels alive. The other person is just a shadow of this one, a shell to hide this one.

"Do we have computer scientists?" Christian asked.

Luke chuckled.

"We're the FBI. Of course, we have computer scientists," Tommy stated.

"We need everything we can get from this profile and his. IP addresses, reroutes, associated names, others contacted. Tell them to get everything."

"All right."

"I'm hungry," the kid said. He stood up and walked down the hall without so much as a glance at the two of them. Tommy stared without moving until Christian stopped ten feet away. "Is there someplace to eat around here?"

Tommy looked at Luke. If Christian's face had shown intense interest a moment ago, Luke's held mild approval.

"Sure," Luke said. "There's a sandwich shop around the corner. Mind if we join you?"

Tommy watched Christian's eyes widen as if the idea had never occurred to him. He had been expecting to eat alone.

"Yeah, that's fine," he agreed a second later.

Tommy shook his head, a smile on his face. He had two weird partners, and he'd never understand everything they did.

Two footlong subs sat in front of Christian. He pulled one out of the wrapper and started munching on the first section. He always asked that they cut his subs into quarters. He never understood why they only did halves. If the knife was next to the bread, why not make two more cuts? It made holding the sandwich easier.

"You're going to eat all of that?" Tommy asked.

Christian looked up from his sandwich. He hadn't forgotten that two other people sat with him, but his mind wasn't concerned with them.

"What do you mean?"

"That's two feet of sandwich. You're about a hundred and fifty pounds, Christian. I'm not sure you'll survive both of those."

Christian saw the smile and, a second later, realized it was a joke. He smiled too and looked back down at his sandwiches.

You eat more in a single meal than most people do all day, his mom had said years ago.

"I, um...I eat more in a single meal than most people do all day," he said, still smiling as he thought about his mother.

"I can see that." Tommy laughed.

Christian glanced at the six-inch sub Tommy held. Then he looked at Luke, who had a chopped salad in front of him.

"Hey, if you're hungry, eat," Tommy said and took a bite of his sandwich.

Christian did as he was told.

Don't go inside your head, Melissa told him. She spoke from behind the restaurant's counter. *You're here with people. You should make conversation.*

He knew she was right, but his mind wanted to focus on the case, the criminal, and the killings. He also knew she would keep talking if he didn't do as she asked.

"So," he said. "I think this guy was abused pretty badly as a child."

"Do you?"

Christian heard Luke ask the question, but he didn't look up, just kept munching.

"Yeah," he said through a mouthful of food. "I'm not sure if it was the mother or the father or both. The whole household was violent is what I imagine. That's where the eyes come from."

Christian had no clue that the entire table had stopped eating, both of his partners staring at him.

"That's why he cuts them out," Christian continued. "Eyes can show a lot of emotion, or at least that's how we view them. The eye isn't really showing the emotion. It's the face around the eye. Yet, when he *removes* the eyes from their heads, the emotion disappears, and all that stares back at him is a sort of purity. Perhaps even a truth. That's what he's after. He wants people to look at him as pure like he views himself, a good person. His parents' eyes showed a lot of disapproval, and he doesn't want to see that anymore."

Another bite. He chewed it, thought about speaking again, and took another mouthful before talking.

"I don't think he deals well with disapproval nowadays. We're looking for someone who, if they get a bad writeup at work, will make a scene. He doesn't need perfection. He just needs people to act like he's perfect."

"Hey, Christian," Tommy said. "You mind if we just eat for a minute?"

Luke knew it was time to start. Perhaps past time, if he wanted to have maximum effect, which he did.

He put his bag down on the kitchen table and pulled out his personal laptop, leaving the FBI-issued one inside. It was just before midnight, his group having finished going over all of the reports that came in thirty minutes ago. A lot of tips, none of them good. Interviews had been completed by other investigators, but nothing promising had come out. While they hadn't told the Yorks that their daughter had most likely been murdered for her eyeballs, Luke knew it was true.

Tommy would break the news to the parents when they had proof.

Would he bring Christian with him? Tommy was taking an unusual role with the boy, a sort of fatherly apprentice-ship. Luke thought it interesting if silly. Tommy wasn't married, though, nor did he have any kids. Luke knew he saw a woman once or twice a week. He had stood outside Tommy's apartment downtown and watched the woman leave one morning. Pretty, with red hair. Tommy never mentioned it. Luke checked up on her—Alice Stromin. It was good to know about those that you worked with, especially given what Luke had planned.

He typed in the social network website they had visited earlier. The three of them had debated whether to reach out to the killer's profile, but in the end, they had decided against it. They were working on acquiring a warrant for the social network and would have a yes or no on that by tomorrow morning, which meant Luke needed to act tonight.

He stared at the man's face, knowing that whoever was

on the other side of that profile looked similar but not exactly like the picture. The picture had to resemble the killer so he could get close without alarming the victim.

He loaded his encrypted TOR browser. It took the necessary steps to ensure no one could track him physically or digitally, then he went live on the dark web.

Luke reloaded the website inside the TOR application, created a fake profile, and located the killer again.

His fingers hit the keys with nearly magical rapidity, flying across them while he closed his eyes and listened to the keys snap back. He found the sound of typing musical.

Finally, the letter was done.

Luke hit send, then closed the laptop, placed it in his bag, and went upstairs to his bedroom. He laid down and fell asleep immediately.

Bradley's eyes were open. He gave up trying to keep them closed an hour before, knowing that he wouldn't fall asleep regardless of what he did. Bradley had hurt plenty of animals, his mother, and his father, but he had never felt an urge like this. The *need* to do it again was driving him insane.

He had killed two people in a week and wanted to kill another.

That was how you got caught.

Bundy had done that stupid shit, going through that sorority house as if he might never get another chance to kill someone. Bradley wouldn't do that. Couldn't do that, not if he wanted to keep living on this side of a prison cell.

But what the fuck was he supposed to do? He couldn't sit in here and not sleep for a month. Tomorrow would be hell at work, no doubt about it, and he *still* needed to talk with Charlie about their last conversation. He didn't want to have that particular talk while exhausted, though.

What do I do?

He could go out and kill someone, but that would be stupid, especially without planning. The first two pairs of eyes had been planned out, one from a bar, one online, but he hadn't set up anything else yet.

Maybe you're not so smart. Maybe Father was right, and you are an idiot, regardless of what your IQ says.

Fuck that, he thought. You showed him how smart you were in the end. How dumb he was, too.

"Okay, okay," he said, trying to push the angry thoughts out of his head.

His computer screen flashed on across the room, lighting up the darkness. Bradley squinted as his eyes adjusted, trying to see what the screen signaled. A notification. He had left the notifications on when he was dealing with the York girl, wanting to be able to answer her immediately if she messaged. He hadn't looked at the messages since he froze her downstairs, though, and there hadn't been any others as far as he knew.

Yet, the screen was on, and Bradley could see a message waiting for him.

He climbed off the bed and padded across the room, then sat down at his computer.

A new name sat in Bradley's inbox. Or a moniker, because no one was named Johnny Consultant. He clicked the notification, and the message popped up on his screen.

Delete this account and everything associated with it. Wipe your computer. Contact me through Signal messaging. My number is 555-4646.

That was it.

Nothing else.

Even the picture in the top right corner gave Bradley nothing, only showed a large magnifying glass.

Someone knew?

"That's impossible," he said. "Even if they have the conversation from her end, there's nothing that would lead to me."

He stared at the screen, mouth open, unable to believe what he had just read. Someone knew who he was, and if Johnny Dick-Sucking Consultant could figure it out, the FBI would have no problem.

What do I do?

Bradley grabbed a sheet of paper and a pen from his desk and wrote down the phone number. He knew Signal was an end-to-end encrypted messaging app. No one would be able to read anything sent over it, not even the company that owned the application.

Bradley closed his eyes tight, forcing the screen's light from his mind. He felt a headache threatening to overtake him. He hadn't had one since his father died, which had ended and started a lot of things for him, but he remembered that they were crippling.

He opened his eyes and flew through the necessary screens to delete his account. When that was done, he clicked his mouse a few more times, and a message popped up.

Are you sure you want to reset to factory settings? This will delete all files and programs not originally associated with the computer.

Bradley clicked yes.

He went to bed but still couldn't sleep. The migraines were back.

CHAPTER TWELVE

"Thanks for meeting with me, Agent Phillips," Veronica said.

"Not a problem, though I'm not sure how much help I've been," the FBI agent, Tommy Phillips, said.

He was cute and smart, though not as smart as Luke Titan. Veronica doubted she'd ever meet anyone else as smart as Titan, or if she did, that they would have the ability to communicate their intelligence in a way others could understand.

"Would you mind if I contacted you again if something else comes up I'd like clarification on?" she asked.

"Not a problem. Luke said to talk freely with you." Phillips stood from his desk, following Veronica's lead. The interview had lasted about an hour. After Veronica had her first meeting with Titan, she had spoken to her agent about the book. Veronica strongly suggested that while focusing on the Sphere, they should take a pro-Titan angle.

The man is captivating, Veronica had said. *Readers will love him.* Her agent had agreed, and the scope of the project had expanded, allowing her to gain needed insight into Titan's life.

"Yes, Dr. Titan is being great about this. Can you suggest anyone else here I might find it worthwhile to speak to?"

"Well..." Phillips glanced down at his desktop, then looked back up. "His first partner might be a good idea. He's no longer with the bureau, but it might give you a different perspective than mine."

"Oh, great. What's his name?"

"John Presley."

It took Veronica two days, but she was finally able to locate John Presley and arrange a meeting with him.

He worked for one of the jurisdictional courts now. She couldn't find out what he did, and he was vague about it when she reached him on the phone.

She found out what he did when she showed up at the courthouse.

"Oh, John? Sure, come with me."

The courthouse was fifty miles outside of the city and didn't appear to get much business, at least during this time of day. One of the clerks at the front desk, a kid who was maybe in his early twenties, probably in college and doing this part-time, stepped away from his charge and led Veronica down the hall.

"Not a lot of people come by here unless they have a parking ticket or something. It's a pretty small town," he explained as she stepped up next to him at the security station. A single guard stood beside a brown wooden table with a metal detector in front of it. "If you have anything in your pockets, go ahead and take it out. Julie here will push them to the other side of the metal detector."

Veronica did as she was asked and made it through the detector without any issues. They took the elevator down to the basement floor.

"Okay," the kid said. "Here's John's area. Just head to the back, and he'll be sitting in his office."

Veronica's head tilted slightly sideways as she looked at the clerk. From what she could tell, they were in the basement. "His office?"

"You'll understand when you get there," the kid said and smiled. "Have a good day."

The elevator door closed, and Veronica stood in something that looked like an old library. The ceilings were low, and she saw no windows. Books—at least they appeared to be books—sat in tall cases to her left and right, rows of them.

"Hello?" she called.

"I'm back here."

Veronica followed the voice, walking past empty tables as if someone might come down here and pull out one of those books for an all-day study session.

"Over here," the voice said, and Veronica looked at her right.

An older man sat in an office with much more light than what was out on the floor. The door was open, and she walked inside.

"Hi, I'm Veronica Lopez. You're Mr. Presley?"

"Yes, ma'am." He stood up, and Veronica put his age somewhere at fifty plus, maybe early sixties.

"Nice to meet you," he said, extending his hand. "Welcome to my domain."

"Mr. Presley—"

"John, please," he interrupted.

"John, what do you do here?"

"I'm the recordkeeper. They're slowly moving everything to digital, but this is one of the last counties in the state to go that way, so they're employing me until it's completed. If you need the history of a case that took place here, I'm the man you see."

Veronica turned halfway around and looked out the office door. "I don't mean any offense, but this is very different from being a special agent with the FBI."

"It is."

She turned back around. "Do you enjoy it?"

"Some days. Have a seat, and we can talk."

The two sat down, and John continued. "It wasn't how I saw my career ending, but then again, I didn't see myself meeting Luke Titan either. That's who you wanted to discuss, right? You're writing a book about him?"

"Not him specifically, but yes, he's going to be a major part of it."

"What do you think so far?" John asked, a dry smile on his face.

"He's a genius. I was as shocked to find him in the FBI as I am to find you here."

"Because he's too smart to be an agent, and I'm too smart to be a recordkeeper?" John asked.

"Well, I wouldn't put it like that."

"But it's true. That's okay. I *am* too smart to be here, but to understand whether Titan is too smart, you have to ask why he's at the FBI in the first place."

Veronica pulled out her phone and loaded the recording app so that John could see it. "It's okay if I use this?"

"As long as my name isn't used. You can use the words I say, but they can't be attributed to me. I'd like that on the record, too."

Veronica pressed the record button. "My name is Veronica Lopez, and any information gathered during this interview will be used anonymously in this or any future published works. Sound good?"

John nodded. "So, where would you like to start?"

"First, how did you come to meet Luke Titan?"

"He was assigned to me when my last partner retired."

"You were *his* first partner, correct?"

"That's right," John answered.

"How was it working with him?"

"In the beginning, it was fine," he said. "The end, though? You can see how it worked out for me."

Veronica nodded, her interest piqued. Phillips had been right. This would give her a different perspective. "I can't find any public records about you, John. I don't know what happened at the FBI, and I don't know why you're here."

"That's how I want it. I'd rather not have the world know Titan's version of events, given that I still have to live in that world."

"Were you fired?"

"I retired," John said. He looked past her at his office's window, and the dry smile returned. "That's the official wording. I was forced out and told that I was lucky to avoid jail time."

Veronica said nothing as his eyes met hers. She'd wait until he was ready to continue.

"We, Titan and I, were tracking a pair of credit card thieves. They were operating all over the country, stealing identities and using the money to buy whatever they wanted. A little more sophisticated than bank robbers, but not much. I ended up killing one of them. He was unarmed."

"How did that happen?"

"The truth or the official report?"

"Both," she said.

"Well, officially, I discharged my weapon to use deadly force without provocation. The truth is just as simple, even if I can't prove it. Titan drugged me. He'd been drugging me during the entire case. There are doctor's records of the problems I was having. Midnight hallucinations. Passing out. Horrific migraines. They put me through a battery of tests, but everything came up negative. They didn't know what they were looking for, though. That's why they never found it."

"Hold on a second," Veronica said, leaning forward. "You're saying your partner drugged you, and in the end, you were so deeply under the influence that you ended up shooting an unarmed man?"

"No, I ended up killing an unarmed man. I'll never be able to legally carry a weapon again."

"Did you tell anyone else about this?" Veronica asked.

"Of course, once I understood what was happening. I was jailed for two weeks after the murder. Titan couldn't get to me then, and the drugs wore off. The hallucinations ended. No more passing out. Everything simply stopped at the end of those two weeks."

"That doesn't mean he was drugging you, though."

"It certainly doesn't. All of this is circumstantial and sounds crazy. I know that. My murder case moved slowly through the FBI, and I started researching when I was released from jail. I obtained the original blood samples that were drawn at the time of the incident and had them rerun, looking for contaminants that were present then but weren't now. I previously worked drug enforcement for the FBI, so it made sense that something could cause such massive deviations from reality and end just as quickly."

"What did you find?"

"Broken-down compounds," John said. "It was perfect how he did it. Those compounds could not be traced back to him. He used a derivative of LSD. Low dosages at first, acclimating me to it. The day we went to make the capture, I imagine he used a pretty heavy one."

"Listen," Veronica said. "I'm not trying to call you a liar, but I took LSD in college. There isn't any way that you could have gone to make an arrest while on that drug and not have known."

"It's a derivative compound. I've done a lot of research into this, Ms. Lopez, and he combined it with hypnosis compounds as well."

"And he told you to kill the man?" She didn't believe that. This guy was sitting in this basement because he'd killed an unarmed person and wasn't able to handle the aftermath. John Presley had cracked, and this was the result. The old man was unable to come to terms with what he'd done, so he'd made up an excuse.

"Yes, he did. He screamed, '*Shoot him. He's got a gun!*' I saw the gun, and I shot him."

"Why, Mr. Presley?" she asked, putting separation between her and the man by using his last name. "Why would he do something like that?"

"I never figured that out. Maybe you can with your book."

CHAPTER THIRTEEN

Luke looked at the application on his phone. It was an incredible tool, brought about by government overreach, no doubt. Complete encryption so no one—not governments or the CEO of the company that made the app—could read what was said.

The government's overreach had created more talented criminals.

The message had come in at five this morning. Luke had been awake. The television was on in his living room, the morning program discussing a movie that was about to be released. Luke hadn't been paying attention to it. His mind was elsewhere. Sometimes he found himself lost in his thoughts. He'd always been like that.

The past often crept up on Luke, though he rarely regretted anything. He sometimes wondered if his past drove him as it did so many others. For all the things in this world that he could answer, he didn't have one for that question. Perhaps it did, or perhaps he was the master of his fate. Either way, he saw no reason to change course now. Too much past behind him, he supposed.

The app's notification pulled him from his thoughts, which was good. He would need to head to work in the next thirty minutes but had been hoping that his new friend would contact him first.

Who are you?

Luke looked at the number that sent it, memorizing it instantly. He would run analytics on it later, privately, and see if anything came up. Most likely it wouldn't, not if his new friend was intelligent.

I'm someone that wants to help.

Do you know who I am?

I know what you're doing, though not who you are.

A minute passed without a response.

How can you help me? Why do you think I need your help?

Luke smiled. How long would it take Christian to understand the insecurities plaguing their killer? Had he already figured it out?

Maybe you don't, but then again, I found you online. If you don't need help, you can disappear and act like this never happened.

Another minute passed, but Luke didn't place his phone down. His friend was hooked, only deciding how to respond.

How can you help me?

I can help you see around corners.

Luke hit send and then placed the phone down. He went to his bathroom, disrobed, and stepped into the shower.

"I'm going out, Mother," Bradley called through the door.

"Is there anything to eat?"

Thank goodness, the old bag was finally hungry. Bradley had begun to worry that she might try starving herself to death. Having a dead woman in his house wouldn't be good for him right now, especially not his mother.

"Yes. Do you want me to bring it in or leave it out here?" He needed to treat her better. He needed to be nicer because regardless of how she acted or what she had done in the past, she was his mom. She gave him life, and he had no other family outside of her. He was going to try to be better.

"You can bring it in," she said.

It sounded like she wanted to try harder, too.

Good, he thought as he headed to the kitchen. The meat from the girl was gone, but he still had peanut butter and jelly. He thought about how he'd eaten the girl as he fixed Mother's sandwich. He'd been repulsed at first, the mere thought making him gag.

What forced him on was the "No body, no crime" mantra he knew he had to live by. All that was left was a small plastic container of broken-down bone. Bradley hadn't been lying to Charlie when he'd said he'd boiled the bones, though he had lied about eating them as broth. That would have been far too barbaric, even for Bradley's purposes.

No, he had used a pressure cooker and put the bones in it with bleach, which had caused the structural components to fall apart. It'd taken time, and he worked outside at night due to the fumes, but eventually, he had finished the entire body. All he needed then was to take a small hammer to them, and they shattered like glass.

He would dump the plastic container while he was out today.

No body, no crime.

Except for the eyes, Bradley. Don't forget about those.

No one was coming here. He was too smart for that, even with the headaches returning.

Bradley pressed the top of the sandwich down, then sliced through the middle.

The headaches would be a problem if he didn't get them under control. He wondered if this fucker who was texting him had brought them on, the added stress causing it. They used to come when his father was around, doing his awful deeds.

Bradley carried the sandwich to his mother's room and opened the door slowly. The darkness nearly swarmed out, a stark contrast to the rest of the well-lit house. He walked over to her bed and placed it on her lap.

"Here you go."

"Thank you," she said. She stared out the window, not reaching for the sandwich but not pushing it away either.

"Do you think you might want to come out of your room tomorrow? Maybe we could rent a movie or something? I'll turn it up so you can hear everything."

"Yeah, maybe we can do that," Mother said.

He looked at her for a few more seconds, unable to see much of her face given the way her head was turned.

"Okay," he said finally. "I'll be back in a few hours."

Bradley left the room and then the house, careful to lock up everything. He didn't lock Mother's door, of course, because she couldn't go anywhere without his help. She knew that, too. One thing about Mother—Bradley figured he could thank his dad for it—was that what happened inside their house stayed inside their house. She wouldn't bring in anyone from the outside.

Bradley wasn't stupid, but the person texting him might think he was. Bradley received an address, and the text had said, **You'll love what you see**. Bradley had gotten a slight erection from the text, though he would never tell anyone that. Especially not the prick offering help.

Bradley didn't even drive by the address. He had looked it up online, then spotted four different places from which he could watch it from a distance. Now, he drove to all four of the spots, his car moving at a normal pace so as to not gather too many wandering eyes.

Ha! That was a good one.

He didn't see anything out of the ordinary, but that didn't mean someone wasn't watching him. He finally parked his car at a mall ten miles away and started thinking. It would be a clever way for the cops or the FBI to catch him, but if this person did want to help, it would make things a lot easier for him.

The message hadn't said when to go to the address or what to look for, but that didn't mean the FBI wouldn't have twenty-four-hour surveillance on the place.

Bradley got out of his car and went into the mall. He walked to the food court but didn't buy anything. He sat and watched people walk by, doing his best not to stare too closely at any of their eyes. He didn't want to be distracted. He needed to focus on whether or not to actually go to the house.

Six hours later, he finally emerged from the mall.

He couldn't help it, he decided. A headache was coming on, and if Bradley didn't do something to stop it, he wouldn't even be able to drive home. Just like with his father, he knew how to kill the pain. Whatever was at the address might help.

"Fuck 'em," he said as he started the car. He'd go right up to the goddamn doorstep. Even if they were watching, they couldn't prove anything. The number he used was from a burner phone, not attached to him. Bradley didn't even have a cellphone. Everything was in his mother's name, and they only had the landline.

He parked the car in the driveway. The house was old,

single story, and not well kept up. If Johnny Consultant had bullshitted him and made him waste an entire day, Bradley would take out *his* eyes. They wouldn't make it to the freezer, though. No, Bradley would eat the damned things.

He walked up to the front door and lifted his hand to knock, then saw that the door was open.

"What the..."

He tapped on the door, and it swung open.

"Hello?" Bradley called into the house.

No response.

He couldn't help himself. He was here and the door was open, so he went inside. He moved through the house slowly, looking at everything. Someone old lived here. The furniture, the television, the appliances—all of them had been purchased a long time ago, and their owner had been on a budget.

He found her in the back bedroom.

The old black woman was tied to her bed, her arms and legs attached to ropes that were wrapped tightly around the bedposts. Another rope went over her torso and then under the bed, trapping her.

Bradley looked out the bedroom door, checking the hallway. No one was here.

He looked at the woman, who had a gag of some sort in her mouth, though she was struggling to make noise.

Bradley heard none of it, though. All he could see were the beautiful blue eyes in that old black face.

CHAPTER FOURTEEN

"This is our guy," Tommy said as he stood next to the bed. "No doubt about it."

Ten years ago, he would have vomited at the scene before him. Even now, he felt his stomach turn over.

"Looks to be the case," Luke said from the other side of the bed. "Christian, would you mind telling the police to ensure the perimeter is completely secured? Tell them to let us know if the media arrives, as well."

"Me?" Christian said.

Tommy looked at him, standing in the bedroom doorway.

"Sorry, kid. You're going to have to learn to talk to people in this job. It won't be hard," Tommy said.

"It'll be harder than the hardest erection you ever had," Christian said.

Tommy had turned back to the bed but flashed back to Windsor at the comment. The kid was smiling, which brought one to Tommy's face as well.

"A joke," Christian said.

"Go on, get out of here."

He listened to Christian move down the hallway and focused on what lay on the bed. The woman's name was Ida Clarey, and the house records showed she had lived here forty years. She was seventy-three or had been. Now she was dead.

"He's getting sicker," Tommy said.

The eyes were gone, of course. Two dark holes stared out of a wrinkled face. That was the only part of her that hadn't been harmed, if the removal of someone's eyeballs could be considered unharmed. The rest of her body was...

"He's mutilating them now. It's different from the first victim. There he just cut the head off. This is..." Luke's voice trailed off.

"Far worse."

The woman's breasts had been sliced off and shoved over the bedposts, one on each. The bottom-left bedpost had been broken off and protruded from between the woman's legs. Tommy didn't want to look at it, but he had to. She was naked and her groin bulged, her body not made to fit what was now inside her.

"What's this mean?" Tommy asked. He didn't expect an answer from Luke or anyone else. It meant nothing, and to give it meaning was to give credit to the monster. It was meaningless, as was the monster's existence, regardless of what *he* thought.

"It could be anger," Luke said. "Or he's just messing with us."

Tommy looked over the bed at his partner. "Let's hope he left something."

Luke didn't look up from the ravaged body. "Let's."

Christian stood between three forensic scientists. They worked in silence, which was good since he didn't want a lot of people talking to him. Not ever, but especially not right now. He wanted to look at the body, and though he couldn't do it alone, he *could* do it in silence.

This was savage, more so than even the first murder. The killer had acted differently here. No eyeballs lodged in orifices. This time, he had left something much more painful.

Why? Christian wondered. He walked over to the bed and knelt next to the body, not noticing the look one of the scientists gave him.

"If I touch the cadaver, that's okay, right?" he asked without looking around.

"We'll need to print you for exclusion, but yes, as long as you don't change its position."

Christian nodded and slowly placed his hand on the woman's arm. Her skin was wrinkled. It had been through a lot, and she had met her end in one of the worst ways imaginable. "Was she alive when everything happened?"

"She was alive for the bedpost and the breast removal but dead before the eyes."

Christian didn't need to ask how they knew. The cuts were far too neat for her to have been alive while her eyes were removed.

"What are you?" he asked.

"What?" a tech asked him, but Christian didn't hear.

He stared at the woman's black skin but didn't see it. He

was inside his mansion again. He stood in front of the door marked Surgeon.

This man should be called the Demon, not the Surgeon, he thought, and opened the door.

A chair was pulled out for him, with nothing else around it. A large leather thing that was meant to be comfortable because what Christian was about to witness wouldn't be. He sat down, knowing what came next, or at least the process. He had tried explaining this to his mother once, but she said she didn't need to know how his mind worked. Only that it did.

Christian sat down in the chair, slumping because he didn't want to see the movie that would show the Surgeon.

He brought one hand to his brow, half-hiding his eyes.

"I can't run from this," he said, though his voice traveled only inside his mansion. "Not if I want to help. That's why I joined. To help."

He didn't remove his hand, and the movie began playing.

Inside Christian's head, the connections to the killer were being formed.

Christian sees a young boy. His face is blurred, but that was because Christian hasn't yet formed the connections to see what the boy looks like—or the man who is now a killer, for that matter.

The boy is naked. He is about ten years old. He's out in the open, on a field of some kind, with no one else around.

Christian can't see any clothes, so the boy must have walked here this way.

He's standing over a primitive trap, a wooden box with a piece of food in the middle of it. The box's front door was attached to a stick that had been placed next to the food. When the field rat moved the food, the door slammed shut.

Christian sees the boy peering at the rat. It is pressed into a corner, looking up at the large creature, clearly terrified. There is no sign of the food that had been there.

A name is screamed across the field, but Christian can't make it out—another problem with the still-forming connections. The boy looks in the direction of a house. It's maybe a mile off. The boy had walked a long way out here to see this rat.

"LUUUUNNNCCCHHH!"

The boy's mother has called him.

The boy looks at the rat for another second. Finally, he squats, the sun shining on his bare back, and opens the box. He looks at the animal, the two as close as they will ever come. He then stands and takes off across the field.

———

Christian closed his eyes and took a deep breath. The movie paused, allowing him to take in the information. His unconscious mind had categorized and analyzed it, but his consciousness needed to understand it to help him make the needed leaps.

"Okay," he mused. "You weren't born evil."

Is anyone? he wondered.

Christian didn't want to go on, even more so now than

when he'd first entered. The boy let the animal go; he hadn't tortured or killed it. He knew that what came next wouldn't be as nice because something had turned a boy who would free an animal into a person who would shove a bedpost into a woman's vagina.

"Catch anything?" the faceless mother asks. Christian can see nothing more of her face than he can the boy's, except her eyes. He sees those clearly, but he doesn't need to. He already knows the color, which is blue.

Christian stands at the kitchen doorway. The boy is inside the kitchen, and the mother's arms are elbow-deep in soapy water at the sink.

"No," the boy lies.

"That's two days in a row," the mother says.

"I don't know why."

The boy is still naked, and as the mother turns around, Christian sees for the first time that she is too. Both boy and mother stand without clothes, looking at one another.

"Your father isn't going to believe you," she says.

Bright red streaks up the boy's neck into his face. Christian knows what the boy did. He had opened the box's door, but the wooden stick had been tripped and the food eaten. All his father needed to do was walk out to the box to know the boy was lying.

The mother watches the rising red across her son's face and knows what it means. The boy is lying.

"You tell me right now. Was there an animal out there?"

The boy nods.

The mother rushes across the kitchen, her naked breasts swinging as she does. She grabs the back of the boy's neck, and Christian sees sinewy muscle popping up across her forearms. The woman is strong. The boy tries to cry out, but her other hand clamps over his mouth.

"Your father is out working all goddamn day to put food on this table, and you're going to free some rat? That's how you repay his hard work? It's time for you to start carrying your weight around here." She speaks with a calmness that contrasts harshly with the underlying hatred in her voice. "Give me your hand."

The boy extends his arm upward. His hand is shaking horribly.

The mother rushes him across the kitchen to a chopping board on the counter. She moves quickly, like some kind of animal herself. Like the rat that had huddled in the corner of the box. One of her hands grabs a large butcher knife from the holder next to the board. She raises it above the boy's wrist.

"So, we'll eat *you* tonight. How does that work for you?"

The boy is crying and saying he's sorry. That he didn't want to hurt the animal, and he won't disappoint her again. His penis has shriveled and is indistinguishable from the flesh around it.

"Do you want us to eat you?" she asks in that same calm voice.

"No," he blubbers.

Christian winced, his eyes shutting again as the movie turns off. He didn't want to continue.

"I want to go home," he said.

You can't, Melissa told him. *You have to see this if you're going to help.*

He knew she was right and opened his eyes. The movie resumed playing.

The boy is still naked, though Christian is watching him on a different day.

He's in the field again, in front of the box. A rat is inside, perhaps a different one than the time before. Or, maybe it's the same, a rat that couldn't learn from the lessons of the past. Or maybe the lesson the boy taught it was that the box was safe. Someone would free it.

Christian doesn't think anyone will free it this time.

The boy squats and opens the door. He looks for a second, then says, "No one's going to eat me."

He reaches in, his hand moving like his mother's had, quick and ruthless. He grabs the small field rat, and the thing squeals and bites his hand.

This enrages the boy. The thing is attacking him. It isn't his mother. It isn't his father. What right does it have to bite him? Especially after he freed it, or at least one of its brothers.

The boy brings the rat to his face, standing up as he does. A tiny bit of blood wells where the rat's teeth are lodged in the skin between the boy's thumb and index finger. The blood slides down the inside of his hand, meeting the rat's fur. The animal doesn't stop struggling, and the boy hardens his stare.

"No. No one's eating me. We'll eat you."

Christian knows the boy considers biting the thing's head off for a brief second, but... *What will Momma think?* he wonders, and Christian hears the thought as clearly as he heard the mother's call for lunch earlier.

The boy reaches up with his left hand and twists the rat's neck. It stiffens briefly and then goes limp in his hand. The body is still warm, and the boy doesn't release its head right away. He stands there, staring at the blood leaking from his hand.

Finally, he removes his left hand and sees the rat lying still over his thumb. He squeezes the body slightly, watching it puff up above his closed fist. He squeezes harder and sees the dead animal's tongue protrude from its mouth.

"You bit me," he says and squeezes even harder. Its eyes are bulging now.

Don't mess up dinner, a part of him thinks. *Not if you don't want to be eaten.*

The boy turns away from the box and runs back across the field. He's smiling as he does because Momma and Daddy will be proud.

CHAPTER FIFTEEN

Christian placed the sub down on Tommy's desk.

"Only one today?" Tommy asked.

"I didn't want to listen to you making fun of me," Christian said. He didn't look up, so he didn't see the smile cross Tommy's face. He thought Christian was joking.

"Hey," Tommy said. "I was just kidding. You can eat whatever you want."

"You're going to give him a complex," Luke said from the chair in front of Tommy's desk.

"Okay," Christian said. "I'll eat what I want. Listen, we need to talk." He looked around for another chair and found one at the small table in the corner of the room. He pulled it over, leaving the sandwich on Tommy's desk.

They had left the crime scene three hours ago and were just now meeting. Christian didn't know what Luke and Tommy had been doing, only that after he left the body, he went to his apartment and lay on his couch. He hadn't turned on the television or even any music. He laid in silence and thought about what he'd seen.

"Well, what do you want to talk about?"

Christian looked up, realizing he'd been sitting in silence for a few seconds, lost in his thoughts.

"It's not going to make sense how I know the things I'm about to say, but I'm reasonably confident they're true."

"What's reasonably confident?" Luke asked.

"Ninety-two percent."

Tommy laughed. "Okay, let's hear it."

"I think the person we're looking for has some scars, and they're from abuse. I think one or both of his parents is dead. If it's both, we need to start looking in foster homes, orphanages, and juvenile detention centers for someone with scars who was in the orphanage perhaps ten years ago. If only one parent is dead, we need to look at farms that went under in the past ten years. The farms are going to be south of us."

"Slow down there, champ," Tommy said. "What the hell are you talking about? We can't just start sending out manpower on hunches, and that's what I'm gathering this is."

"It's not a hunch," Christian said and met his eyes. "It's correct, and we need to send whatever we have to investigate the leads."

Tommy looked at Luke. Christian could feel the other man staring at him.

"Tell us why you think that," Luke said.

"I can't *explain* it. I've never been able to explain it. If I have to try, I guess I'd say the anger we saw with the last woman was the catalyst. He's mad at someone. He's harboring a lot of anger at that person, and it exploded on the old woman. Also, people don't just start cutting off..."

Christian paused, uncomfortable with the next word. "People's breasts without reason. No, this guy has seen some very bad things, and not in the movies. He wasn't born like this. He was made."

"Luke?" Tommy asked.

"You two look into it. I'll stay with the interviews."

———

"Don't you get tired?"

Tommy closed the car door as Christian got in on the other side. "What do you mean?"

"You work longer hours than anyone I've ever seen," the kid said. "You're here before I am, and you leave after me."

Tommy smiled. He'd heard things like this since his youth, and the answer was always the same. He started the black sedan and reversed. "Christian, look at who I'm working with. You and Luke. Both of you are two of the smartest people in the country, and I'm supposed to contribute. Now, *you* might be crazy. I'm not sure yet. It really depends on what we find when we start looking into your theories, but if you're right... Well, I'm going to have to work even harder if I want to keep up. I don't have the mind you two have, so I use what God gave me."

Christian was silent as the car rolled out of the parking structure. Tommy said nothing. He liked being around the kid. There was a certain comfort that came with his unease as if Christian was worrying enough for everyone, so Tommy didn't need to, which was a first for him. Luke never worried about anything, so Tommy had to. The price of security is insecurity and all that.

"You don't think I'm right?" Christian asked after they'd traveled a few miles. They were heading to the Department of Social Services to look into orphanages. The farms would come next.

"I don't know," Tommy said. He paused, but he knew Christian wanted him to continue. "I don't know how you can be right. We all saw the same things in there, and three hours later, you came back with your theory. Luke didn't think of it. I didn't think of it. Nothing in that house suggested it."

"If I tell you something, do you promise not to laugh?"

Tommy glanced at the kid, but he was staring out the passenger window.

"Yes."

"There's a place I go inside myself. It's what separates me from most people, I think. My therapist says it's both real and symbolic. It's real in the sense that my mind can hold almost anything I want it to. It's symbolic in that it allows me to be different in a way I can't out here.

"Like right now. I hate wearing shoes. I hate shoes, Tommy. They're like casts for your feet. Why do I need to wear a cast on something that has evolved to be the perfect instrument for walking? My skin would grow calluses, and my bones and tendons would toughen. I wouldn't need shoes after the first two weeks, but here I am in my mid-twenties, wearing them everywhere I go. Inside my head, I *never* wear shoes. Does that make sense?"

"Sort of?"

"That's fine. 'Sort of' works, I guess," Christian continued. "When I go to this place, I can find anything I've ever seen, and when my subconscious works on things while

I'm sleeping or concentrating on something else, it shows them to me when I return. It's like watching a movie, to be honest. Well, when I saw the body this morning, I went inside and watched the movie. What I saw was a boy that was abused on a farm."

Tommy remembered his promise not to make a joke. Christian was looking at him, and his face said he needed Tommy to understand. Perhaps not believe but understand.

"I don't have a place like that in my own head, but I do in real life. When we're done here, do you want to see it?"

"Are you playing with me?"

"No," Tommy said. "I'll show it to you."

"Okay," Christian said. He stared out the window.

Luke's new friend had taken quite a few liberties with the woman Luke gave him. He hadn't expected such savageness. Luke had, of course, spent a lot of nights over the past week figuring out which person he would give his friend. He settled on an old woman with no family, no job, and barely any outside contact with the world.

She had to have blue eyes, though. Luke needed to know if the color mattered or if the friend was simply creating a kaleidoscope of eyes.

The color mattered. Not the skin tone or the age, or even the relative beauty. The eye color.

Luke stood in front of the body's head. The pathologist, Roger Linson, was on its right side. Roger was almost finished with the autopsy, but Luke wanted to see if his friend had slipped up during his rage and left a fingerprint or something.

So far, at the house, they found no fingerprints but five different sets of hair. Three were cats, one was the old woman, and the last an unidentified person—most likely Luke's friend, which was careless. For Luke's needs, the friend had to be very careful. Mishaps early on would end Luke's goal prematurely.

"Did our perpetrator leave anything? Semen, finger-prints, a written address where he can be found?"

Roger grunted and moved away from the table to the sink. He pulled his gloves from his hands, trashed them, and started washing his hands. "No. There were smudges from the blood on the severed breasts indicative of a latex glove. The woman wasn't raped, either before or after death, so no semen inside her. I'd ask the techs if they found any in the house. A lot of times, guys will bust their load while they're abusing someone."

Luke hated talking to Roger. The man said the simplest things, as if he were the only one who knew a killer's psychology and Luke couldn't possibly figure out that he should check the crime scene for semen as well. Perhaps one day, Roger could fit into his plans.

"All right, thanks," Luke said.

"There is one thing."

Luke was on his way out the door, but he stopped, holding it open. He knew Roger loved doing this, holding him up just as he was about to leave. Yes, Roger would find his way into Luke's plans at some point.

"Yeah?"

"I found a partial eye lens."

"Where?"

"Come back in, and I'll show you."

Luke let the door close and returned to the metal table. Roger pulled out a light and shined it into one of the eyeholes.

"When you remove an eye, if you go deep enough in the cavity, you'll touch the brain. There was an eye lens there. I haven't run DNA matches, so I don't know if it's the woman's, or not conclusively. However, there were traces of water on it, which leads me to believe it isn't the woman's. I think it had been frozen."

Luke ignored Tommy's call.

He wanted to concentrate on his friend. Perhaps he wasn't as careless as Luke originally thought. He had brought the eye lens with him and placed it where it might never be found. Even when Roger removed the brain, it was too small to be noticed.

That was a thank you, Luke thought. A "thanks for your help."

It also meant his friend was more trusting than he portrayed. He brought the piece of eye with him to the house, meaning he thought Luke's offer might be legitimate.

That was good.

Trust meant Luke could do more.

And there was *a lot* more to be done.

"What about that movie?" Mother asked.

"Not right now. I have a headache."

Bradley picked up the plate from his mother's bed. It was past one in the morning, and she was in here asking for a goddamn movie like he hadn't just worked all fucking day. Not work that she would respect, though. No, now that Father was dead, she was a damned saint.

"Tomorrow?"

He looked at the old hag and knew his migraine would disappear if he strangled her to death right now.

She hadn't turned toward him, of course. She never did. Not since... Well, since what Bradley had done to her.

"I don't know right now."

He turned away and walked out of her room, needing to get away. If he didn't, he'd kill her. He would do *anything* to make sure his headache didn't return. It had to be from that damn Johnny Consultant. There wasn't any other reason for Bradley to be having migraines. He hadn't felt like this since before his father died. Years and years.

Bradley didn't bother taking the plate to the kitchen. He dropped it in the hallway and went to the garage. It took him a second to turn the lock because his hand was shaking so badly. This headache was going to be a real doozy if he didn't do something about it quickly.

He felt his phone vibrate in his pocket. Bradley didn't reach for it since he didn't care what the damned message said. If it couldn't help with this migraine, the person could go fuck themselves.

Bradley went to the deep freezer and opened it up. Two plastic bags sat inside. He grabbed the one on the right, the newest, and pulled it out.

Eyeballs stared back at him, glossy with frost.

A slightly different shade, he thought. Bradley looked back down in the freezer and thought about grabbing the other bag. *No. Not yet. Not until the room is finished. Those are to be the last.*

He wasn't going to rush things, regardless of how badly his head hurt. And the migraine was going away, wasn't it? Just holding the eyeballs, even through the plastic, helped tremendously.

He took the eyeballs out of the bag, then shoved it into his pocket. He would dispose of it later by burning it in the fireplace. He needed to empty the fireplace to ensure no evidence was left, but that could wait.

He took the eyeballs to the pair sitting in the middle of the room, and with great care, pierced each, shoving the needles through the frozen flesh. He pinned them to the wall above the first pair.

"Oh, it looks beautiful, Mother," he said, not aware he was speaking to his mom. "Father would love it. He'd see the truth in all of them."

Bradley hadn't worn a jacket into the garage, and the cold was getting to him. His teeth chattered, and his breath came out of his mouth in white plumes.

"Oh," he whispered.

He bent to the eyeballs and gave each one a kiss, his lips sticking as he pulled away.

CHAPTER SIXTEEN

"You promise not to laugh?" Tommy asked.

Christian nodded but said nothing. His face held the look of someone who had taken a long pilgrimage and was finally about to reach what might be the promised land. The voyage had been hard, but hope lurked just under his tired face.

It was ten at night, and Tommy turned the car's lights off. They had switched out the black sedan for Tommy's personal car, and now they sat in front of his condo.

"Let's go up, then," he said.

They got out of the car and walked inside the building, taking the elevator up to Tommy's floor. He was nervous that Christian might think this was a joke, but it wasn't. Not to him. He'd told Alice, his girlfriend, how he viewed this place, but no one else.

They stepped outside of the elevator and walked down the hallway. Tommy took his key out and opened the door to his condominium. "Come on in."

The two walked inside, Tommy leading.

"This," he said, "is all I have to compare to what you told me."

Christian stopped walking, standing in the living room. Tommy continued walking, stepped around the coffee table, and sat down on the couch.

"Do you see?"

He watched as Christian looked around the room. What was he noticing? What was he picking up? Would the kid tell him to fuck off and storm out? How great was his perception?

Christian walked to the wall and looked at the single picture containing people. It was of Tommy and his mother; his father was nowhere to be seen. That had been true for much of Tommy's life.

"Your mom?"

"Yes."

He moved to a painting. Two elephants, a mother and her baby, in profile with the sun setting behind them.

"And this?"

"I got a thing for elephants. If there was any justice in this world, they'd rule us instead of us ruling them," Tommy said.

Christian nodded and stared at the painting for another second. Finally, he turned to Tommy.

"This is your mansion."

"Probably not as nice as yours, but yes. It's my place of solitude. I don't get the insights you do, but I can block out the rest of the world when I'm here."

"What else?" Christian asked.

Tommy smiled. The kid wanted to know more about him. He could sense that wasn't the only thing Tommy wanted to express by bringing him here. "Do you call what you have a sixth sense?"

"I don't call it anything. Other people do."

Tommy nodded. "You're different because you can't communicate well with others. I was different because I couldn't stop working. Even as a kid, whatever goal I set, I worked all day and sometimes all night to hit that goal. I didn't have friends. My mother encouraged me, but I think it bothered her. Sometimes I got picked on until I set a goal of learning self-defense. This is the first home I've ever owned, and I won't sell it because it's the first place I've been able to feel truly safe. Does that make sense?"

No tears glazed Christian's eyes, but Tommy thought he saw something there. Perhaps identification with a kindred spirit.

"It does."

Tommy didn't say anything for a few seconds, just looked at the kid. "You want to sit down?" he asked finally.

"Sure."

Christian went to the love seat catty-corner from the couch. He was quiet as he sat.

"You want to talk about today? We can fill Luke in tomorrow."

"Okay," Christian said. Tommy would have sworn on a Bible that he saw a switch flip inside him. One moment he was contemplative, perhaps feeling emotion that he couldn't quite express, and the next, it was like a machine took over.

"Go on," Tommy began. "Clearly, you have thoughts."

No smile. "I think one parent is still alive. There are still a few places we need to check, but one of them lived, and that kept him out of state care. He lived on a farm, though. I'm fairly certain of that."

"There aren't any farms around these parts, in case you didn't know."

"Yeah, but in case you didn't know, people move," Christian shot back, the smallest grin pricking his mouth. "So, they moved here at some point, but why would they do that? The only reason I can think of is they lost the farm, so we need to look at bankruptcies."

"How many farms went bankrupt in the past twenty years, Christian?"

"A lot. I haven't looked at the exact number, but we can probably narrow it down to a five-year window."

"That's still a hell of a lot of bankruptcies."

Christian shook his head. "I don't think he has a heavy accent, so we can throw out the Deep South."

"Would that be racism? Classism?"

"It's elimination. Don't start with me on the politically correct police. I could go for years complaining about them."

Tommy laughed. "Okay, okay. We'll focus on small farms in southern Georgia. How will we know when we find him, though?"

"I can't figure that out yet. I'm hoping that when I see it, I'll know."

"That's not going to work with the director. We need something more solid."

Christian leaned back on the loveseat and closed his eyes. "I need more time around him or around what he does. I need more connections."

Tommy stood and walked into the kitchen. "You drink?"

"No."

"Ever tried it?"

"No."

"Well, I won't start someone's alcoholism. I'm going to have a beer. You want to stay the night? I can drive you home if you want, but it's not a problem."

Tommy listened to the silence as Christian wrestled with how to answer the question. Tommy knew he wouldn't want to spend the night. Asking him to do that was akin to asking a normal person if they'd like to ride a bucking bronco. The fear alone would keep him away.

"Hey, just thought I'd ask. Let me finish this beer, and I'll drive you home."

"You're going to drink and drive?" Christian called from the loveseat.

"There's a lot I need to teach you."

***

Tommy dropped Christian off. He watched him walk up the stairs to his condominium, and once he was inside, Tommy pulled away from the curb.

Like you're bringing home a date or something, he thought as the car rolled onto the freeway. Tommy felt a certain duty to the kid, though he couldn't pinpoint why. Or rather, he knew why, and if it was anyone else, this wouldn't make sense. The kid was a duly appointed FBI agent, had two doctorates, and clearly was capable of doing anything he wanted in this world. Yet, Tommy hadn't pulled off immediately. He made sure Christian got inside.

Because, as smart as he is, he needs help in this world. Hell, you needed help too, and you ended up getting it.

Not from his own father, but yes, he had gotten help at a time in his life when he needed it. Maybe that was what he was trying to do with Christian.

Tommy didn't get off at his exit but went back to the office. It was late, but he wasn't tired, and there was a pretty big snag in Christian's theory, even if he thought he'd be able to see around it eventually. They couldn't comb through farm bankruptcies, hoping to somehow magically land on the name of the man who was doing all these killings.

They needed more than that.

He pulled into an empty parking space and exited the car. It took him five minutes to make it to his office. The place was empty, the lights turning on as he walked through the silence.

Tommy hadn't been lying when he'd told Christian he worked so hard because he had to if he wanted to keep up, but that wasn't the only reason. He enjoyed the work. People were dying, and he could make it stop.

He fired up the computer and started working. They would need more than Christian's sixth sense if they wanted to catch this guy.

CHAPTER SEVENTEEN

Luke sat in his car and looked at the house in front of him. A nice house. A respectable one. Something someone worked a long time to pay off. A place that could keep them safe because the neighbors were friendly, and the police patrolled the area.

John Presley had done well for himself by American standards.

It was unfortunate he couldn't keep his mouth shut.

Luke's last conversation with Veronica Lopez had been quick. She called him with some follow-up questions, telling him she was expanding his role in the book given the importance she thought he deserved. Luke agreed, although he didn't say so.

Yet, John Presley came up in one of those follow-up questions.

"So, on the record, you didn't poison John Presley?" she had asked.

"I don't even feel that justifies a response," Luke said.

It didn't. Of course, he had poisoned John Presley.

There were many ways Luke tried to go about his business. They didn't all work. John Presley's hadn't, and so Luke abandoned it. He was, though, working swimmingly with Tommy and now Christian.

But John hadn't been able to stay quiet. Veronica went over the gist of what he said, and Luke might have underestimated the man. It seemed he did a hell of a lot of research after he blasted that credit thief.

It wasn't that Luke needed to do anything to the man, but he *wanted* to. No one was going to listen to John Presley, not before and not now. Still, Luke was going to pay him a visit at his nice house. He'd see his nice wife, his nice life. All of it predicated on a man who kept his nose to the grindstone and worked hard. That might have been true, but what the American Dream didn't account for was the role of chance.

Luke *was* chance. A slight tremor on an otherwise still craps table, something no one would notice but moved the dice *just* enough. Snake eyes. No payout.

Luke stepped from his car. He pressed the button on his keys, locked it, and gave it a look. It really was a nice car. Elon Musk knew what he was doing with Teslas.

Luke dropped the keys in his pocket and walked across the street. He didn't cut across the lawn, but walked up the driveway, then took the concrete path to the doorstep.

He rang the doorbell, the glue he'd applied to his fingers earlier in the morning ensuring that he wouldn't leave a fingerprint.

The street was still dark. Some people were awake, but no one was heading to work yet.

It took a few minutes, but Luke didn't mind waiting. He

enjoyed the cool morning air and the silence around him. Finally, John Presley spoke through the door.

"What are you doing here?"

"I was hoping we could talk about what you told Ms. Lopez."

Luke wore one of his suits, ready for work when this nasty business was over.

"What do you have to say?"

"Well, if you let me in, I'll tell you. I think it might be best to clear the air between us."

"Give me a minute," John said.

Luke waited in the stillness. He felt serene as a breeze blew through his hair.

The door opened and John stood in front of him, wearing a robe and holding a piece. A 9mm.

"That might not be the best way to start the conversation," Luke said.

"Fuck you. What do you want to say?"

"I wanted to talk to you about your conclusions and see if I can convince you that I did poison you, but it's best if you stay quiet about it."

John's mouth opened, his lips parting.

Luke moved more smoothly than a striking serpent. One hand grabbed the man's mouth, brandishing a handkerchief soaked in chloroform. The other grabbed John's right thumb, the one holding the weapon, and pulled back. He tried to scream, but Luke had control of the situation.

The gun fell to the floor, and John Presley went limp in his arms.

Luke wore a pair of sweatpants and a sweatshirt. He had put them on under his suit for this specific purpose. He had put on gloves too, latex ones. He wasn't worried about fingerprints, but you could never be too careful about hair follicles. On his head, he wore a swimmer's cap, pulling it down so that it covered everything but his face.

He had scrubbed his face earlier this morning, ensuring that any skin or loose hair wouldn't fall off. If they did, Luke's eyes were *extremely* perceptive.

John Presley sat on his couch. His hands were bound to his ankles, all of it tied so tightly that he couldn't move. He had fallen on his side during his temper tantrum, and now he lay there with blurry red eyes and a rag shoved deep into his mouth.

His wife was on the floor in front of Luke. Had her eyes not been blue, Luke would have needed to figure out another way to take care of John, but sometimes Luck smiled down from her cloud.

Mrs. Presley's eyes sat in a little plastic bag which rested next to the television.

He'd made John watch, of course. Luke took his time with the woman, having already planned out what he would do before showing up. Of course, it needed to look like his friend had been here, so Luke contemplated what drove the man. It hadn't been difficult. His friend's psychology wasn't much different from that of other psychopaths.

Luke had cut the woman's tongue out while she was awake. He had then taken each of her fingers off with a pair of bolt cutters, blood spurting on the white living room carpet. The blood had soaked Luke's clothes as well, but that wouldn't be a problem.

Finally, he'd sliced the woman's throat, nearly severing her head. John had watched from the couch, trying to scream but unable to make any noise.

It took about an hour.

People were finally starting to move around outside, heading to their jobs.

"Now," Luke said, "I won't take as much time with you. I do have somewhere to be, after all. We're really busy trying to catch 'the Surgeon,' as the media has branded him. Do you know why they call him that?"

John didn't even look over, just stared at his dead wife, unable to pull his gaze away.

"You're in shock, John, but that doesn't mean you can't continue learning. They call him the Surgeon because of how precise he is with his removal. It truly looks like something a doctor might do. Anyway, we've got a lot of work ahead of us, so I'll need to be moving along."

Luke stepped over Mrs. Presley and stood in front of the silent Mr. Presley. A single tear dripped from the man's eye, rolling down the side of his face before it swelled and then fell to the couch.

"You should have kept quiet, John. I wouldn't have called on you. I've always wanted to hurt you, but when you left the FBI, I thought my opportunity had passed. You did this. I want you to know that. You killed her. You brought me here, and you didn't have to."

Luke reached forward with the knife and slit the man's throat.

He moved back, making sure none of John's blood touched him. He didn't want any more filth on him than necessary.

133

CHAPTER EIGHTEEN

"Four murders in two weeks is a big fucking deal, guys, in case you weren't aware."

Director Alan Waverly stood in the former FBI agent's house alongside Luke, Tommy, and Christian.

"I don't need to tell you that I don't have time to be here, looking at this, right?"

Christian didn't know if the other two needed to be told, but he didn't. "I don't ever want to be around you."

The other three men looked at him, their eyes wide with surprise.

"I mean… I mean," Christian stammered, "that you being here isn't a good thing for us. It means we're not doing our jobs. I meant that I don't want to be around you because I want to be doing a good job."

Waverly blinked twice, his eyes slowly returning to their normal size. He turned back to the crime in front of them.

From the corner of his eye, Christian saw Tommy fighting a smile.

Glad someone finds my issues humorous.

"I need answers, gentleman, and I need them fast. What can preliminary forensics tell us?"

"Not much." Luke was standing on the other side of Waverly. "No prints, no loose hair. Nothing that points to anyone besides the two of them being here, at least not in this area. There were other hair samples and prints that don't match Mr. and Mrs. Presley, but we imagine that will show up as friends and family."

"You're running them, though?" Waverly asked.

"Yes, sir."

"This was your former partner, correct?" the director asked.

"Yes, sir."

"You don't seem too broken up about it."

Christian watched Luke. He wasn't looking at Waverly, only staring at the bodies.

"We weren't close after everything that happened."

Christian blinked, much like Waverly had moments before.

What is it? he asked himself, his brain firing so hard that it almost physically itched. *What's bothering you?*

Stay focused, Christian, his mother said. She was only in his head this time, thank God, not standing over these disgusting bodies. *You know how you can be sometimes, allowing your mind to take you off the task at hand. Now's not the time to do it, especially with your boss's boss standing here.*

She was right. He blinked hard one more time and cleared his mind.

"Do you think he's after you?" Waverly said.

"Would be an interesting way to go after me, given what this man accused me of."

Silence fell over the room, and Christian wasn't about to break it.

"He killed one of ours," Waverly said. "Even if Presley did leave under difficult circumstances. If it wasn't personal for all of you before, it better be now."

More silence. Christian didn't know how to act. Was it normal for the director to say something and everyone around him to keep quiet, or was this different because of the person murdered?

Honey, focus, his mother reminded him.

"Use the normal protocols with this. Look at everyone around these people and see who they knew, who talked to them recently, et cetera. If we find nothing, we have to believe one of two things: either he stumbled across this woman because of the blue eyes, or he's targeting people you know."

"I don't have much family," Tommy replied.

"Mine isn't even in the country," Luke added.

"Windsor?" the director asked.

"My mom." Fear struck his spine, nearly paralyzing him. She wouldn't be harmed. Couldn't be. No matter what.

"Twenty-four-hour watch on her from now on, okay? Until we know more about this. Is there anyone you two would like surveillance on?"

"Can I get back to you?" Tommy said.

"Of course. Now, what leads do we have?" Waverly asked. "Tell me you've got someone you're looking at."

Christian was about to let Waverly know the theory,

but Tommy started talking, giving him a sidelong glance as he did.

"Yes, sir. Windsor did some work, and we're targeting people who had farm foreclosures between ten and fifteen years ago."

"Why?" Waverly asked.

"Evidence left at the last crime scene," Tommy said. He didn't look over as he lied but kept his eyes on the director. "We've kept it out of the press, but it was in the report we sent a few days ago."

"And the evidence was…"

"Not evidence, per se," Luke spoke up, "but it gave us a direction to go in. The brutality shown on the last victim made Windsor start digging through criminal profiles, and we think the killer was abused as a child. Now, in horse rearing, when they breed… Well, the stallion has a very large male organ. The bedpost had been whittled down, carved to make it resemble a—"

"A horse's cock? Are you fucking kidding me?"

"No, sir." Luke didn't look away from the bodies. "He took his time in that house while the woman was tied up."

"Jesus Christ. I need more, guys. How are you going to know it's your man when you find him?"

"Last night, I started combing through farm foreclosures and cross-referencing them with victims of child abuse. So far, I haven't found anything. I'll be looking again tonight," Tommy said.

"I'll have some of our interns do it for you. Listen, don't hesitate to ask me for resources on this, okay? Whatever you need, call me directly. No reason you should be doing that. Just look at the reports the interns give you."

"Yes, sir."

"Call me tonight, both you and Luke. Christian, since you dislike me so much, no need for you to be on that call."

Christian could barely hold his eyes up, but he saw a small smile cross the director's face. Perhaps other people would have been miffed that they weren't required to be on a call. Christian felt only relief.

Director Waverly left, and the three men stood alone at the crime scene.

"You two...lied."

Luke, his eyes on the dead, said, "We're a team. It won't matter in the end as long as we catch the guy."

Christian loved the picture behind his psychiatrist. It let him keep his head up but not have to look at her. He stared at it now, trying to decide whether to discuss the case. He wasn't here to work on work but on himself, yet he couldn't let the crime scene from yesterday go.

"It wasn't like the others," he said.

"What wasn't?" Melissa asked.

"The murder."

Melissa was quiet. Christian could see her despite not looking at her, and he knew she wanted him to continue without prompting.

"I don't know why it was different, though, and that's what bothers me."

"You'll have to be a bit more descriptive, Christian."

"This is how you're helping me today, huh? By making me express myself in ways people understand?"

"People understand you just fine. I'm not concerned with whether they do or don't, though. What I'm trying to do is make you work on the things you don't want to work on because my job is to help you reach your potential."

"Most people would say I've far surpassed my potential, given my age."

"Maybe theirs," Melissa said, "but not yours. Now, go on. Describe what's bothering you."

He sighed and finally met her eyes. "For one, the man who was murdered had a problem with one of my partners years ago. You've seen the news. One of the victims was an FBI agent. That right there is *different*. The second thing, I guess, is that there were two people present. He was violent with the wife, but the man got off fairly easily. He only slit his throat."

"Easy if you don't consider the horror of watching your wife's mutilation," Melissa countered.

"True," Christian mused. "I didn't think about that. But why would he make the man watch? That's even more of an issue because it creates unnecessary risk. Your victim could escape and stop you."

He shook his head. "No, the killer wouldn't have had two people there. If he did, he would have killed the man first."

"How do you know he didn't?"

"Blood patterns. The woman's blood was spilled first."

Melissa grimaced.

"Sorry," he said. "We can talk about something else."

"No, it's fine. So, are you thinking there's a copycat?"

"That doesn't feel right either because of the *eyes*. They were taken with the same precision as before. No difference. That's my guy. There's something with him and eyes that I don't fully understand, but there's not another serial killer with that kind of skill."

"Well, Christian, either there *are* two killers with that skill, or your guy did it."

Christian was unsatisfied, to say the least. He couldn't remember the last time something had bothered him this badly, but then again, he couldn't remember the last time he hadn't been able to solve something.

He sat at his desk across the floor from Tommy's office. The light was on inside, and the blinds had been drawn. The rest of the floor was almost empty, and the janitorial staff had begun their rounds.

Luke walked out of his office and caught Christian's eye. He started over.

What happened in that house yesterday? he wondered. *What was that itch you shoved away?*

"Burning the midnight oil?" Luke asked as he arrived at Christian's desk.

"I'm getting hungry, but yeah, I'll be working late."

"Want to get something to eat? I'd ask Tommy, but he's worshipping at the altar of Workaholism right now. We can go back to my place after if you'd like. Work some there. I need some space from this office if I'm going to think effectively."

Christian's eyes narrowed as something shot into his mind. He couldn't see it well, though, like a flare that flamed out before fully igniting.

"Everything okay?" Luke asked.

"Yeah. Yeah. Sure, I'll grab dinner with you. How late do you want to work?"

"The way Tommy and I look at this is, if the killer isn't sleeping, we aren't either."

"You're not too worried about gaining weight, I take it?" Luke said.

"I'm not sure I can."

The two sat in Luke's basement. They weren't near the whiteboards but sat in the leather chairs that faced the television, which was turned off.

"Have you ever seen a dead body before this case?"

Christian shook his head and took a sip of the coffee Luke had made when they arrived. He was full from the five-egg omelet he'd eaten and needed the coffee to help wake him up.

"What do you think of them?" Luke asked. "The bodies. Do they make you feel anything?"

Christian blinked. "I'm not sure I see them like you and Tommy. I see the man behind it. I feel pity for him, I think. He was hurt a lot."

"Does that mean he's guiltless?"

"No, of course not," Christian said, looking into his coffee mug. "It doesn't mean we can't understand him, though."

The two were quiet as Luke took a sip from his mug.

"How did you make so much money?" Christian asked.

Luke smiled and looked around the basement. "Well,

I'm almost in my forties, and before the FBI, I did pretty well in the private sector. Did well in academia, too."

"This is your third career, then?"

Luke nodded.

"Do you think you'll have another one?"

"I don't know. I'm not motivated by money. I never have been."

"What does motivate you?" Christian asked. He felt something different from what he felt when he spoke to other people, even his mother or Melissa. Energy seemed to float in the room, and Christian didn't know if it sprang from him or Luke. It was there, though.

"Can't you tell?"

"I haven't given you much thought. I'm preoccupied, I guess."

"What about Tommy?" Luke asked. "Have you given any thought to him?"

"No, but I don't think he's as complex as you."

"Or as complex as you," Luke countered.

"I'm not that complex." Christian didn't like the conversation's turn. He didn't want to focus on himself or how he did what he did anymore. He'd explained it enough, more than he ever had before. "Let's not talk about us. Did you want to discuss the case?"

Luke nodded, and Christian looked at him. His brown irises were small against his large black pupils, seeming to fill most of his eye. The light above them cast shadows on his lean face, and Christian was shocked to see beauty in the man—not in a sexual sense, just admiration. He hadn't noticed it before.

"How are we going to catch him, Christian? I'd like to know what you think."

Christian couldn't pull his eyes away from Luke's even though he wanted to. A kind of magnetism kept him staring. "You want the truth?"

"You seem very good at telling the truth. To a fault, many would say."

"I'll keep seeing his crimes until I know as much about him as he does. He'll continue killing, most likely increasing the speed, and we'll get him. We'll narrow down who he is until a body tells us more than he wanted it to."

"What will happen to him once he's caught?" Luke asked.

"What do you mean?"

"Death penalty? Insane asylum? You think we'll kill him in the act?"

"I hadn't thought about it," Christian said. "What do you think?"

"He's not insane, not in the form a court will accept. Does he know the difference between right and wrong? He certainly knows whether society deems what he is doing is right and wrong, or he wouldn't hide it so well. If I had to guess, we'll kill him before he ever goes to trial."

"Why do you think that?" Christian asked.

"Tommy."

Christian cocked his head, confused by their partner's name. "He's not violent in that sense."

"Not usually, no, but you don't know what happened to his brother. This case holds a special place for Tommy, even if he doesn't talk about it."

"What happened?"

Luke looked at the television for a second. "You want me to tell you, or do you want to ask him?"

"You tell me."

Luke paused for a few seconds. "You should know, given what we're dealing with. He has experience with this in a way that neither of us ever will. His brother is still considered missing, but that's because the body never turned up. Tommy was sixteen, and his brother was twelve. He went to play basketball one evening and never came home. I'm surprised you didn't create a dossier on both of us, to tell the truth. Surprised you don't already know this."

Christian was too, now that he heard it from someone else's mouth. "You think a serial killer got his brother? You think he might see this man as a way to avenge his brother?"

"I wouldn't go that far," Luke said, "but I don't know what will happen when he's in front of him. Maybe something switches inside his head and the killer gets killed. Wouldn't be a bad thing, would it?"

<hr>

The Uber rolled quietly down the highway as Christian sat in the back. He looked out the window at the streetlights, which were passing too fast to see them individually. He wasn't trying to focus on them, but rather thinking of the couple of hours he'd just spent with Luke.

It's his intelligence. That's what I'm drawn to. That's why I feel different when I'm around him.

He hadn't understood that until he was out of the man's

presence. It was a feeling that he hadn't ever experienced and one he wasn't comfortable with.

And what he'd shared about Tommy? Should he have done that, or was that something for Tommy to share when the time was right?

Christian didn't know the answer to that question. He constantly overshared. The social etiquette of others baffled him more often than not. Yet, Luke had shared something personal with him, even if it was about someone else.

Am I looking for a friend? he wondered.

If he was, if he thought Luke Titan might be that person, what was the problem? Why question it? Couldn't he have friends like everyone else?

What had happened in that victim's house?

The question rose unbidden to the top of his mind. He couldn't push it away, not forever, even if he wanted to. His mind wouldn't let him. It would pester him until he faced it.

Not right now, he thought. *It's too late.*

And it was. The Uber stopped in front of his apartment, and at four in the morning, Christian finally found sleep.

CHAPTER NINETEEN

"Thanks for meeting with me again," Veronica said.

Luke Titan sat down at the table across from her. The weather was warm outside, though not hot. Titan had requested through email that they meet at this restaurant and that they sit outside when she reached out to him about Presley's death.

"Not a problem. How can I help you?"

"Well…" Veronica paused as the waiter came over.

"Hey, do you guys know what you'd like to drink?"

"Just a coffee, no room for cream," Veronica said.

"I'll take a vodka tonic. Double shot, tall glass, please," Titan said.

"Okay, I'll be right back."

Veronica looked across the table. "Double shot during a lunch hour? Don't you have to go back to work?"

"My metabolism is very fast. It's a gift and a curse. I can't put on weight, but I can process alcohol quicker than most." He smiled as he spoke, and Veronica couldn't tell if it was sexy or chilling.

"Interesting. Are you okay with this being on the record?"

"No. Nothing that we talk about involving an open case can be on the record. I'll talk to you about it, but it can't come out even as an anonymous source, not now, not later. Not without my permission."

Veronica nodded, having figured that would be the case, but she thought she would try, nonetheless.

"The man who accused you of poisoning him is dead, apparently murdered by the killer you're trying to catch. It feels like an odd coincidence, to say the least."

It felt like more to Veronica. When she had seen it on the news the previous night, a cold chill had run across her body, causing the hair on her arms to stand at attention. She had just spoken to John Presley a week ago, and now he and his wife were dead, the woman sans eyeballs.

"I'm not sure I believe in coincidence, Ms. Lopez."

"Would you agree that it's at least odd, then?"

"I can definitely agree to that."

The waiter stopped at the table, two drinks in hand. "Here ya go! Did you two want to eat?"

"I'm okay," Veronica said.

"I'll follow the lady's lead. Thank you, sir," Luke answered.

"You don't seem very surprised or...I don't know, perturbed about this turn of events." Titan was just as calm as he had been during their first interview, as he had been when she called him about Presley's accusations as well. Nothing shook him.

"The surprising part is why John's wife was chosen. We're not sure yet if he knew that I had a connection to

John or if this was purely an accident. We have increased our security around agents' families associated with the case."

"Purely accidental? Wouldn't that be a coincidence?" Veronica asked.

Luke smiled again. "Touché. So, Ms. Lopez, why did you want to have this meeting? Was it to discuss the details of John's murder? I can't tell you any more than I already have."

"No," she said. "I just wanted to see how you were taking it."

"The man accused me of trying to poison him with LSD. I'm not terribly torn up about his death, though his wife's was tragic."

"You don't seem torn up about hers, either," Veronica said.

Titan took a sip from his glass. "The best I can do is catch her killer, Ms. Lopez. What's done is done."

Why are you here? Veronica asked herself. *What were you hoping to get out of this?*

The book was going well, and she didn't need this conversation to keep it moving. She didn't even need to consider John Presley's remarks. They were ludicrous on their face, and without evidence to back it up, what was she going to do? Put unsubstantiated and insane claims in the book?

"I'd be willing to talk about anything else, though," Luke said. "How's the writing? I haven't kept up with the Sphere in a while. What's the status?"

"It's moving slower since you left." Veronica didn't know what else to say. She had come here hoping for...what? That Luke Titan would be destroyed over the man's death? That he would share with her some insight? In ten years of reporting, she'd never shown up so woefully unprepared. She sat awkwardly in front of him without questions for him. Finally, she asked, "You didn't do what he claimed, did you?"

Titan actually laughed. "Of course not. I'm not a Buddhist, and I don't think John Presley deserved what happened because of what he said about me, but perhaps he'd built up a lot of negative karma over the years."

"Agent Windsor?"

"Yes."

Veronica didn't know much about the man on the other end of the phone, only that he was new to Luke Titan's group, and she hadn't spoken to him yet. Well, that wasn't *everything*. She also knew this phone call had nothing to do with her book, and while her agent wouldn't tell her to stop chasing it, her agent *would* tell her she was stealing time that she should be putting into the book.

She knew one other thing: John Presley's death wasn't sitting well with her.

"My name is Veronica Lopez. I'm a reporter for the Atlanta Journal, and I'm writing a book focused on the multi-country project called the Sphere, at least by laymen. Are you aware of it?"

"Yes," Windsor said. His voice sounded clipped, as if something was cutting off his speech.

"Luke Titan played a major role in the project, so he's

becoming a larger piece of my book as well. I've already spoken with your partner Thomas Phillips, as well as Dr. Titan, and I was wondering if you might have some time when the two of us could speak?"

"About what?"

Jesus Christ, what in the hell are you doing, Veronica? This man wants to talk to you about as much as an albino wants a day at the beach, and you don't need him for what they're paying you to do. Let him go.

"About Dr. Titan and your experiences with him. I know that you're well educated yourself. Perhaps you could give me your thoughts on the Sphere?"

"Can I call you back?"

"Um," Veronica said. "Sure. Do you have my number?"

"It's on the caller ID."

"Okay, any idea when you'll call, just so I can clear my calendar?"

"Give me five minutes," Windsor said.

"Sure thing."

The line went dead, and Veronica sat in her home office holding her cellphone to her ear. She looked at the computer in front of her, the page open to the last words she'd written over a week ago. Her deadline wasn't for six months, but she couldn't afford to *not* write. Yet, that was what she was doing.

She put the phone down and stared at the last line she had written.

Dr. Luke Titan is more than respected in scientific circles. Some might say he's revered.

John Presley hadn't revered him, and now Presley was dead.

Veronica hadn't slept in the past twenty-four hours. She was running on coffee and a hunch she didn't fully understand. She was tired but also excited; she hadn't felt like this in years. She hadn't followed a hunch in such a long time that she almost didn't remember what one was.

The past twenty-four hours had been spent researching, not the Sphere, but Luke Titan. She knew everything the internet had to offer, and she also knew that no one else had written a biography on the man. It would only be a matter of time before someone did if he maintained his current pace.

Yet, the internet didn't know much about him.

His resume read like something an engineered human might possess. An M.D. and a Ph.D. He wasn't on Forbes' list of billionaires, but the man had more money than Veronica would ever see.

She might have let it all go, but at five in the morning, she found an obituary.

Trevor Rollins.

He had worked at Harvard at the same time Titan had. Others had died during Titan's time there; mostly students in drunk driving accidents, and one suicide. Trevor Rollins was also a suicide. He was the only professor of his stature to kill himself in the past few decades, from what Veronica could tell.

She had dug deep when she found the obit, trying to learn everything she could about the man.

He was, by most accounts, next in line to be the president of the esteemed university. He was dean of their astrophysics department, and if his resume didn't read like Titan's, it read better than anyone else's Veronica knew.

Yet, he put a shotgun in his mouth and pulled the trigger with his big toe, apparently.

He also left the only red mark on Luke Titan's entire career if one ignored John Presley's accusations.

Veronica called the only source she knew at Harvard and asked if he knew anything about Rollins' death.

"It was a horrible thing," Chris Reel said. "He was a good man."

Chris and Veronica had attended undergrad together at Columbia, and now Chris taught geology at Harvard. He had for the past seven years.

"This is going to sound crazy, but was there any relationship between him and Luke Titan? Do you know who that is?"

"Titan?" Chris almost laughed. "I'm not sure anyone here *doesn't* know that name, even though he's been gone for a few years. Yeah, they had a run-in. I think it was right before Rollins killed himself."

"A run-in?" Veronica asked.

"Yeah. I don't know the details. It was all sealed, I'm sure, but all the faculty gossiped about it. Politics, from what I can tell. Titan was practicing medicine while also working under Rollins in the astrophysics department. Working on the Sphere, I think. From what I heard, Rollins wrote a letter to the university president and said that Titan had to cease his medical practice or cease his work on the Sphere. Splitting his time didn't allow him to do a good job for the students he counseled *or* the Sphere, I think. Too many masters and all that."

Veronica had thought about it for another hour before she'd decided to call Titan's other partner.

Too many masters, and conveniently, one of the masters dies.

It was too damned much, and now Veronica was calling another collaborator to ask…what, exactly? Certainly nothing about the Sphere, despite what she'd said on the phone.

Her cellphone rang, causing her to jump. She looked down and saw the same number she'd just called.

"Veronica Lopez," she answered.

"Hi. It's Christian Windsor. When do you want to talk? Are you in the Atlanta area?"

"I am. When's good for you?"

"I haven't had lunch today. If you buy it, I'll talk to you."

Her brow wrinkled. She didn't know if the man was joking. No laughter came over the phone, though. "Sure," she said a second later.

"Meet me at the Subway on Johnson and 285, okay? I'll be there in thirty."

The line went dead, and Veronica found herself staring at her computer again.

Christian wanted lunch, and given the way everyone ate out at the Atlanta office, he was quickly finding himself with a shortage of money. The reporter, whatever she wanted, would need to pay him with lunch if she wanted to talk.

That wasn't the only reason he was going.

She wanted to talk about Luke, and Christian wanted to do the same.

He stood outside the Subway, waiting for Veronica Lopez to show up. He had found her picture on the Atlanta Journal's website, so he knew who he was looking for.

She arrived ten minutes after he did.

"I'm sorry I'm late," she said. "There was an accident on 285."

"It's okay."

Christian went inside, realizing as he did that he should have opened the door for her. He turned around as she pulled it open. "Sorry. I'm not great in social situations. I should have held the door."

The woman's eyes narrowed, but she grinned. "That's okay."

Christian looked at her for another second, then nodded. He ordered his usual two subs, waiting at the register before realizing Veronica stood next to him.

"You're not eating?" he asked.

"Not all these carbs."

"They have salads, too."

"I'm okay," she said, smiling.

He nodded again and didn't look at her until the cashier asked for payment. The woman handed him a twenty. Christian took the two subs and his cup while she took the change. They headed to a table in the corner. Christian ate here often, and he usually took this table when he wasn't with Luke and Tommy. It was quiet, and there was low foot traffic.

He put his subs down and said nothing as he went to fill his drink at the fountain. Finally, he sat down in front of her.

"I really want to eat, but I don't think that's polite. Let's talk first."

The grin returned to her face. "You're an odd one, aren't you?"

"I'm working on it. I've been working on it for a while."

"Making progress?"

"Melissa, my shrink, says so, but I'm not sure. I think if I told her about this encounter, she'd be appalled."

"Well, I wouldn't worry about it. Nothing appalling has happened."

"So, you want to talk about Luke?"

"Yes. Off the record for now, if that's okay?"

Christian had been studying her closely, even if he wasn't aware of it. His mind finally decided this was abnormal enough to alert him. "Why off the record?"

"I'd rather not say."

Christian looked down at his subs. "Well, you paid for them. Go ahead. Off the record is fine." He opened the wrapper holding his first sandwich, unable to keep his promise of talking first.

"What do you think of Dr. Titan?"

Christian took a bite but didn't bother chewing before talking. "Genius. Not sure about his exact IQ, though I imagine it would rival that of a lot of smart people throughout time. I think history will judge him unkindly for joining the FBI, given the work he did before this. I can't comment on his detective work since I just became one and I haven't worked around him long enough."

The woman didn't say anything for a few seconds, causing Christian to look up. "You *are* an odd one."

"I know. Thanks for reminding me."

The two stared at each other, but she offered no apology.

"I like that you didn't say sorry."

"Why would I apologize for telling the truth?"

"I don't know. I have to a lot."

"What I want to know is your thoughts about him as a person," the woman said.

"Didn't you want to talk about the Sphere?"

"Maybe later. Right now, I'd just like to talk about him, if that's okay."

"When I was younger, the popular kids used to copy my homework. I let them since it kept me from getting beat up. I was rarely hurt as a kid because I was smart, and people needed their homework completed by Monday morning. They used to act like we were friends, but I knew that wasn't true. I did it to keep from getting beat up. There's no threat of getting hurt here, from what I can tell, so I don't see any reason to give you my homework, Veronica."

The woman leaned back in her chair and crossed one leg over the other. "Okay. Fair enough. What do you want to know?"

"I don't need your credentials since you're on the *Journal's* website, but I do want to know why you're asking."

"You're pretty smart, right? Will you be able to tell if I lie?" she asked.

"I don't know."

"I *am* writing a book on Titan and his Sphere," Veronica said, "but I've found some things that make me question his narrative."

Christian placed his sandwich down. "What's his narrative?"

"How well do you know him?"

"I met him a few weeks ago."

"Did you know John Presley accused Dr. Titan of sabotaging his career?"

Christian said nothing, suddenly uncomfortable with the situation.

"Someone else who criticized him died, too. Years ago, when he was in academia."

"I have to go," Christian said. He stood and walked out of the restaurant, leaving the two unfinished sandwiches on the table.

Christian went back to the office and sat at his computer.

He checked the voicemail on his office phone, but none waited. The woman hadn't called him again, which was good since he wanted nothing to do with her or what she was selling.

Why?

You know why.

He knew what his mind wanted to focus on, even if *he* didn't want to.

John Presley's house and the thoughts that had tried to surface inside it. The alarm bells he hadn't heeded, that his mother told him to push aside because something had been *wrong* in that house beyond the two dead bodies.

Christian just didn't know what.

Then think about it, dolt. If you think about it, you might be able to figure out exactly what bothered you. Clearly, it had something to do with what this woman insinuated.

That Luke murdered people who criticized him? That didn't make sense on any level.

Then why did you get up and leave the restaurant?

Because she was crazy and hinting that Luke had murdered people was more so.

But he couldn't believe that, even if he wanted to. Christian hid from the world, but he never hid from the truth.

Are you doing that now?

As she watched the young man walk out of the restaurant, Veronica decided she was done chasing this silly hunch. There was nothing to it, and she'd only push people away if she continued. She might have needed Christian Windsor for her book, but now he was pretty much off-limits.

And if he went back to Titan? Told him what she was bringing up? The book wouldn't be dead, but it'd be harder to complete without access to the man.

Veronica sat back down at her computer a few hours later, intent on finishing the chapter. She had other interviews scheduled for the remainder of the week, none of them having anything to do with Titan. Those would focus on the Sphere.

She stared at the last sentence, desperately wanting to add words but unable to.

Because...

Christian Windsor had gotten up and walked away. He

hadn't laughed or smiled or said, "What the fuck are you talking about?" No, he had stood and left. Her statements had *bothered* him, and not because of how close the two were, not after only a few weeks.

Why would they bother him?

Too many questions and no answers. *So start writing, goddammit. Let it fucking go.*

"*UGHHH,*" Veronica yelled. She stood up from the computer and went into the living room. She wasn't in danger of missing her deadline *yet*, but if she kept putting this off? Even so...

This is what a hunch does. It won't let up. You used to follow these things years ago, back when this was fun and not a paycheck.

"It doesn't matter," she told the empty house as she picked up her remote and turned the television on.

She watched mindlessly for two hours, flipping between the news and a daytime talk show, wondering if there was any difference between the two anymore.

When she checked her cellphone, she saw that it had been on do not disturb. Two missed calls stared at her.

Both were from Christian Windsor's office line.

His voicemail was simple.

"Hi. I'd like to meet again. Call me when you can."

CHAPTER TWENTY

Bradley read the messages again.

If you're going to do it again, you should do it soon.

Why?

They will eventually catch you, but if you can get your fill for a while and let the trail grow cold, you may last longer.

They won't catch me.

A thirty-minute silence ensued after that text, and Bradley couldn't take it anymore.

Why are you helping me?

I feel sorry for you. What happened wasn't fair.

Bradley stared at his phone, unable to believe what he had read. How would Johnny Consultant know what had happened? How could he possibly understand the things Bradley had experienced?

Are you fucking with me?

No. I recognize my own. The world may not recognize those who are abused, but it's hard for us to turn away.

Rage grew in Bradley. This man was lying. He hadn't gone through what Bradley had, not even close. This was bullshit, just a way to trick him the way people had his entire life. Fuck Johnny Consultant. Bradley would kill him and cut his goddamn eyes out, and if they weren't blue, he'd cook them in a fucking stew.

I'm not lying to you. I know it's hard to believe, but why else would I be doing this? Putting myself at risk?

Bradley looked at the phone through blurred eyes as he read the message. He sniffed, pulling snot back up into his sinuses. He hadn't realized he was nearly crying.

Prove it, Bradley wrote. **Prove you actually want to help me.**

Okay.

Bradley looked at the woman. She wasn't tied to a bed like last time, and even though he brought his binoculars, he couldn't tell the color of her eyes since she was wearing sunglasses. Johnny Consultant told him where to find her. Bradley had left the phone back at his house, not wanting any interruptions while he studied this woman.

He didn't know anything about her, but she clearly had money. She was well-dressed, wearing a tight skirt and stepping into a BMW. It was just after seven in the morning, and Bradley sat in his car across the street from her house.

Bradley wanted blue eyes, obviously, but he was beginning to wonder if he needed them each time. Originally, he'd wanted to decorate his garage, turning it into a throne room of sorts. He *still* wanted that, but the act of killing was almost as important now. He needed to do it. It...

The car backed out of the driveway and started down the street.

He'd follow her, then decide if he wanted to kill her. He hadn't asked Johnny Consultant her eye color, but maybe he didn't care. Maybe the person on the other side of the texts was right. Maybe he needed to get some of this out of his system. Then he could focus on his collection again.

"Tell me what happened with the other person that died."

Veronica sat across from Christian Windsor in a park this time. She didn't ask why he wanted to meet here but figured it was more private than a Subway.

"It was ruled a suicide," she said. "He killed himself with a shotgun."

"Why do you think that had something to do with Luke?"

"I don't know."

"I read about John Presley," Christian said. "I might have broken some laws doing it because the files are sealed, but it was a ridiculous accusation."

"I spoke to him before he died. He believed it, and the way he said it? Well, it didn't sound ridiculous. He was convinced."

"I'm wasting time," Christian said. "We have a legitimate killer who is likely getting ready to kill again, and I'm not working because I'm here with you. What you're telling me is that a disgruntled former co-worker believed Luke poisoned him, and someone who didn't like Luke years ago killed himself."

"You seem like a smart person, Agent Windsor," Veronica said. "You looked this up before you came here, so you knew what I was going to tell you. If you thought this would be a waste of your time, why did you come?"

She didn't like his tone or the anger in his voice. She hadn't called him. She had made up her mind *not* to call again. To let the whole thing drop, regardless of how much it bothered her.

Christian sighed and swung one leg over the picnic table's bench so he no longer faced her but looked into the distance. "I don't know. I can't figure it out, but something is bothering me."

"And it has something to do with Titan?"

"I think so, yes."

"Does he know we're talking?"

"No," Christian said. "I didn't think it would be a good idea to tell him I'm talking to someone whose premise is that he kills those critical of him."

"I didn't say that. All I did was ask what you thought of him." Veronica wasn't sure she thought Titan had killed anyone, only that she wanted to know more.

"I'm good at understanding people," Christian said as if he hadn't heard her. "I can almost see their past, but with Luke, for some reason, I can't. Admittedly, I didn't try when I first started working with him, but I have been lately and hard. I get nothing."

Veronica's head moved back when she heard that. "You're not making sense."

"I know. You're not the first person to say that. It's okay."

"Are you saying you're a psychic?"

Christian turned to her, eyes narrowed. "No. I'm not a psychic. You didn't do much research on me before we met, did you?"

"No. Like you said, we both have other things we should be doing."

He nodded, then looked into the distance again. "It doesn't matter. I can't figure him out, and whatever was off in that house won't go away. Do you have a plan or anything? Someone else to talk to?"

"There's no plan for this. I contacted you because what happened was bothering me, too. That's it."

"Then this is the plan. Keep writing your book, and every bit of information you find on Luke, send to me."

Bradley watched the woman sit at a picnic table across from someone he didn't know. The man's hat was pulled low on his head, and she still wore sunglasses.

The more Bradley stared at her, the more he decided that perhaps the blue eyes didn't matter this one time. He'd been so fucking busy lately. Busy with the black bitch. Busy with his mother. Busy with work and Charlie. He hadn't been able to focus on cultivating the next person he needed to kill. Here, though, was someone he could hurt. If her eyes weren't blue, maybe he could create a second-tier caste system in his garage.

Ha! He could have the untouchables and the Brahmins or whatever those people called their betters over there.

The woman stood up from the picnic table and walked back to her car. The other guy didn't move, just sat there staring at the trees across the lawn. Bradley raised his binoculars and focused on the man's face. He was pale. Skinny. Nerdy, clearly. What were they doing here together?

Doesn't matter.

The woman's car pulled away, and Bradley decided to let it go. He would visit her later. He had carefully chosen his first two victims, and the third had been a gift. This one could be for him, just something fun where he went inside and did what he wanted. If he decided to take her eyes, all the merrier. If not, no loss. Blue or brown, he didn't see any reason not to kill her.

Bradley had to work the evening shift tonight, so he headed back home to get ready.

He didn't look in on his mother. He'd forgotten about the movie they were supposed to watch. Too much was going on around him to remember what she wanted. After all, she hadn't cared about what he wanted, not until he *made* her care. Not until he showed her that his father wasn't the one in charge. Only *then* did she start thinking about what Bradley might want.

He turned on the television and pulled his uniform from the closet.

Bradley was about to pull his pants over his boxers when he stopped. The television, or rather, the voice coming from it, made him.

He let go of his pants, and they fell on the floor.

"This is the fourth killing attributed to the Surgeon. This time the target was retired FBI agent John Presley and his wife Patricia. While details aren't being released."

Bradley quit focusing on what the bitch said. Had he killed someone *else*? Was he not remembering what he did?

He stepped from his pants and ran from his room, down the hallway, and to the garage. Unlocking it, he stepped inside the freezing room and trotted across to the opposite wall where his collection waited.

Four eyes, right in front of him. He looked at the corner and saw the single eye he'd placed over there.

"Five. That's it. Five total."

He shook his head, not feeling the cold air all around him.

"Would I have?" he wondered aloud. He ran back through the garage and out into the hallway, not even bothering to close the door behind him. Bradley didn't knock on his mother's door but barged in, flipping the overhead light switch on for the first time in months.

"Hey!" she shouted. She turned to him, not trying to shield herself from the newly born brightness. Bradley didn't bother looking at her but only scanned the room to see if he'd left an eyeball in here. If he'd blacked out and forgotten.

He saw nothing.

He stood for a few seconds, mouth closed, then slowly backed out. He closed the door and his mother hollered something from inside, but he didn't care.

This was important. More important than work. More important than anything else at the moment.

He went back to his room, the news program still running, and he listened.

A copycat.

Someone imitating his work, taking *credit*, yet not helping fill *Bradley's* collection.

And this copycat killed a former cop. No, a former *FBI-fucking-agent*.

"I have to get to work," he said, his voice monotone. He stepped forward and turned the television off, then went back to the business of getting dressed. On his way out of the house, he locked up the garage.

Bradley needed to figure out what the hell he was to do next. He needed to talk to Charlie, if for nothing else than to get these thoughts out in the open.

Charles closed his eyes as Bradley walked through his bedroom door.

It was dinner time, but Charles hadn't had an appetite in weeks. He ate, but only because if he didn't, the staff would grow alarmed. He didn't want any extra attention on himself right now because he had made a decision, and now he needed to act on it.

He made it while watching the news a day or so ago. Bradley had dropped him off at the common area without saying a word, and on the television was the news of an FBI agent and his wife having been murdered. The man's wife was missing her eyes.

Bradley's MO, yet the punk kid hadn't mentioned it. Hadn't gloated. Hadn't offered to bring one of the broad's eyes for Charles to look at.

"That's just horrible," Betty had said to Charles. The old bag had picked the chair beside him despite there being countless others available.

Yes, it was horrible. Charles agreed with the old bag on that point, but he thought it also meant something pretty horrible for Charles. It meant the sick bastard was going to kill him. Why else wouldn't he have mentioned it?

Charles had to do something, and he could only think of two options: tell someone or kill Bradley.

"Charlie, how are you doing?"

Bradley didn't sound well. He sounded about as poorly as he had when he threatened Charlie a week or so ago.

"Have you been watching the news?"

Charles nodded even though he didn't want to. He felt like he didn't have any choice when it came to answering this madman. His body simply took over and did what the bastard asked.

"That wasn't me, Charlie. I didn't kill that FBI agent." Bradley wasn't looking at Charles but staring above him at the headboard again. "I didn't take those eyes out. I'm pretty sure of that. Have you told anyone?"

Charles shook his head once, hard. *Fuck, no, I didn't tell anyone, you crazy dingbat.*

Bradley must have seen him shaking his head, though his eyes never moved. "I didn't think so. I just had to check. I'm sure you understand. Someone else is doing this, but I don't know why."

He walked forward and sat on the bed next to Charles' legs. "I don't know what to do. I'm trying to think this through, but I can't figure out what would be the best move. I mean, if someone else is killing people, that could be a good thing, right?" He gave Charles no time to answer, though the old man shook his head anyway. "It would lead the FBI to someone else, but...*I'm* doing this. *I'm* the Surgeon, not that other guy, and that... It bothers me, Charlie."

Charles nodded again.

"I can't bring the eyes here, Charlie. I'm sorry, but it's too risky, especially with the FBI guy dead now. I could, if you wanted, bring you to them?"

Bradley looked over for the first time.

Oh, Jesus Christ. Charles nodded slowly, his body taking over again.

"Okay. We'll do that soon. Look, it's time for dinner. I'll grab your chair."

Charles watched the half-catatonic Bradley get his

wheelchair and bring it to the bed. Watched as Bradley scooped him into the thing and rolled him down the hall to a meal he didn't want to eat.

He felt like crying, but he might not be able to stop. Charles was going to die, and he couldn't tell anyone. This psychopath was going to check him out of this nursing home, take him to his house to show him his ghastly collection, and then, without a doubt, kill him. No one would go into Bradley's house and come out alive.

"There ya go," Bradley said as he pushed Charles' chair to one of the dinner tables. "I'll come get you when you're done. Have to go do some work now."

Bradley walked away, and Charles looked around the table. His eyes were wet. He wished he could communicate with one of these old fogies. Just one. Tell them what was going on, and maybe together, they could plan an escape. No, that wasn't possible. Couldn't happen. These idiots would blab as if their mouths had diarrhea, unable to even help it.

Who else, then? If not your kids, if not the staff, and definitely not the people around you, who can you tell?

And then, as if God had nocked an arrow and shot it into his brain, the answer was there.

Tell the FBI, idiot. Write to them, and make sure the psychopath doesn't know.

CHAPTER TWENTY-ONE

Bradley had no idea what Charlie was doing, and that was a good thing because Bradley had far too much on his mind to worry about anything else. The more he contemplated someone else stealing his glory, his work, the angrier he grew. So angry, in fact, that he couldn't make his way to that woman's house. Not tonight. He'd make a mistake if he tried to do anything now.

He sat in his mother's room. The lights were off, and she was asleep. Her eyes were closed, and as he sat there, he thought it was funny that she still shut her eyelids. She had been his second human subject. He'd removed her eyes a month after he'd removed his father's.

His father hadn't made it through the operation. His mother had, and Bradley was happy about it. He hadn't been saddened by his father's death. The man had been a brute who loved no one, but Bradley thought his mother's death might sadden him. He sat here now, trying to stave off the headache that seemed intent on possessing him. With her so quiet and still, he found he could think a little better while looking at her. Looking at the work he'd done all those years ago.

His mother couldn't see, and Bradley had made that possible. It was something to be proud of, to take someone's eyes and have them still live. That took skill and remarkable attention to detail. It also showed that he was different from his father. His dad would have cut Bradley from groin to sternum if he thought a hundred dollars might be lodged inside his son somewhere.

I'm kind, he thought, *unlike him. I let her live, and all I took was her eyes, which is much less than what she owes me. She owes me her life, but my kindness spared her.*

Then, much like the answer that came to Charlie earlier, a single and all-encompassing idea appeared in his head.

I have to separate myself from the other person. I have to show that my skill is better than his. I have to leave the women alive. That'll show I'm kind. If this other fucker tries to copy me again, he won't be able to.

Bradley smiled in the darkness of his mother's room. The moonlight shining through the window lit his teeth. In the dim light, his eyes appeared as dark holes.

Charles spent the night with his tablet on his lap. He was pretty adept at moving around the interface—user interface, he had learned. It took him about an hour to figure out all of the main people working on "the Surgeon's" case, then, despite his best intentions, he found himself going down a rabbit hole.

Luke Titan was the reason for it.

Charles was amazed at what the man had accomplished in his four decades on Earth. Charles had worked hard and was fairly wealthy before his kids decided to ship him off to this luxurious nursing home, but what he'd accomplished couldn't even be mentioned in the same breath with this Titan fellow.

Finally, though, Charles returned to the business at hand. He'd found his man, Luke Titan, and he felt certain if he wrote to him, all of this would be resolved quickly.

Charles pulled out a notebook and pen from his nightstand. He was sitting up in bed and propped a pillow on his legs, allowing him to bear down a bit more. Then, with the lamp on, Charles started writing his letter to Luke Titan.

Christian couldn't shake the thoughts of Luke, though he needed to. If it hadn't been for that single moment in Presley's house, he wouldn't have been considering any of this. In fact, the whole thing was preposterous, bordering on insanity.

If Veronica Lopez called back, he would tell her he wasn't interested in what she had to say. He trusted his mind too much, but just because he was smart didn't mean he was always right. What had happened in the house had been a misfire, a flare that shouldn't have gone up.

The thought of Luke being a murderer was pulling him away from what he needed to do, which was find the actual killer.

Christian couldn't sleep, and he was tired of staring at

his computer. Tommy had said earlier that the trail might grow cold if the killer didn't strike again soon. Nothing was panning out from the interviews around Presley, and the others were days old without any valuable leads. The first 48 hours in the investigation were the most critical, and those were long gone. Whoever was doing this could simply walk away right now and would most likely never be found.

Tommy had dug deep into the farms and abused children theory. Nothing showed up on farms that had been foreclosed on or sold.

"Sorry," he had said.

Christian had nodded and stayed quiet.

"That's how this goes sometimes. Some murders remain unresolved, the suspect a mystery."

"What do we do?" Christian had asked.

"We wait to see if he strikes again. We keep following tips and leads. Other than that, there isn't much we *can* do right now. He hasn't left us anything to work with, at least not yet."

"He'll kill again," Christian said.

"Most likely. So, we wait."

Christian was sort of angry with himself for allowing Veronica Lopez to take his attention away from the task assigned to him. Angry at himself for not seeing the stupidity of her crazy witch hunt. If it hadn't been for the timing, he would never have entertained it.

Finally, still unable to sleep, Christian pulled himself from his bed, dressed, and got in his car. He drove across town to the restaurant Crystal Hembree had worked at. The Surgeon's first victim. He sat in the parking lot for a minute and looked through the building's windows. There were a few customers, but business probably wasn't brisk this late on a Wednesday night.

Christian got out of his car and walked across the parking lot.

He stopped at the front door, holding the handle. He didn't pull it.

"Did you come here?" he whispered.

Christian hadn't visited this place before. Tommy had patrolled it on his own right after the murder occurred. Christian had spent his time at the crime scene while Tommy interviewed those that worked with Hembree.

He took a step back and found a bench next to the restaurant. He sat on it and the world disappeared, leaving him inside his mansion. Christian went to the only room he hung out in anymore and quickly pulled up Tommy's notes.

Crystal Hembree had worked here for two years. She primarily worked the bar, but she had filled in for other shifts as needed.

Tommy had written, *Regular customers?*

Beneath it were a few names. A woman whom Christian quickly discarded. Two men, Ryan and Liam. Ryan Hollicomb.

Using the digital walls, Christian found the notes regarding Hollicomb. Tommy had checked him out and crossed him off the list of possible suspects. He had an alibi for every night of the week Crystal Hembree went missing. He was a trucker and had been out of state.

Christian went back to the original note.

Liam. No last name. Manager not one hundred percent that was customer's name. Customer was new, not regular.

Asked manager to look through receipts. Will respond if any match last name w/first.

Even as Christian sat inside his mansion, on the bench outside the restaurant, his hands were pulling his cellphone out of his pocket and placing it to his ear. When Tommy answered, he exited the mansion and came back to reality.

"Hey," Tommy said.

"Did Crystal Hembree's manager ever get back to you?"

A pause, Tommy probably trying to remember what information he was supposed to get from the manager. He'd interviewed hundreds of people, and keeping them all separated couldn't be easy.

"Yeah, he did. He told me they had no receipts for him, so he most likely paid with cash every time. What are you doing right now?"

"I'm outside Hembree's work. How can we find out more about that guy Liam?"

"I...um, I don't know. Look, I have someone over right now. Give me a few minutes, and I'll call you right back, okay?"

"Okay."

Christian hung the phone up and was right back in his mansion. He stared at the name again, written on a perfect replication of the paper Tommy had used. *Liam.*

Christian nodded inside the room, and on the bench, he nodded as well. He came back to reality again, stood, and went inside the restaurant.

"Hi, sir, how are you?" the hostess said as he approached her stand.

"Good," Christian said without looking at her. His eyes were casting around the restaurant, trying to find the bar where *Liam* might have sat. "There," he said. "I'll sit there."

The hostess looked where his finger pointed, her eyebrows raising. "The bar is open seating, sir."

Christian said nothing but walked briskly by her.

"You came here, and you would have sat as close to her as you could, at least by the end. She knew you, didn't she?" he spoke to himself, though his voice was loud enough to carry around the bar. The few customers in the restaurant sat in booths, but Christian wouldn't have cared if he stood right next to them.

He took a seat at the end of the bar, and the bartender walked over to see him. "Hi, how are you?"

"I'm fine. I don't need anything to drink." An intensity was growing inside Christian, and he wished everyone would... "Please, just leave me alone and let me sit here."

"Excuse me?"

"Leave me alone." Christian stared at the bartender, a man in his mid-thirties. The guy looked back at him, obviously pissed off. Again, though, Christian didn't care.

"Let me know if you want something," the bartender said, breaking the confrontation and walking back to the kitchen.

Christian looked up and down the bar. Lights reflected through the liquor bottles sitting on the shelves, illuminating them with different colors: pink, blue, and green. A pink light ran around the bar's edge too.

"You sat here," Christian said. "You sat here and talked to her night after night."

He leaned back on the stool and closed his eyes.

There still aren't any faces. Christian is getting closer, but he is a far cry from knowing the person he is after. He can see more, though, and it's because he sits where the killer once did, giving him the insight, even if he's not fully aware of the reason at the moment.

He sees the killer, older than the boy he had watched on the farm. He doesn't know whether he lives on the farm any longer because the killer is in a part of the house Christian hasn't seen. He's upstairs and standing at his mother's door. She's naked, just as she was last time, but the kid has clothes on now. He's wearing a pair of jeans and a white t-shirt. He looks to be twelve or thirteen years old.

"Your father and I are going to a dinner tonight," his mother says. She sits at a vanity mirror, her naked back turned to her son. Christian can see the outline of her right breast as she bends over a drawer to retrieve her makeup.

The kid says nothing. He's staring intensely at his mother's eyes.

Is this where it comes from? Your obsession with them?

Yes, Christian thinks so.

But why?

The kid doesn't look away from his mother but moves out of his father's path without any trouble. Christian hadn't even known the father was coming into the room, but the kid somehow sensed it. Christian sees him now in all his naked glory. He's a strong man who has spent his life on a farm. The muscle might not be detailed, but it's there, and it's firm.

You're used to getting out of his way, aren't you?

The father walks purposefully across the room. He is, Christian can tell, a man who always walks with a purpose. This time, the kid's mother is what he's after.

The father grabs the back of the chair and spins it as if no one is sitting in it. The woman lets out a small squeal but shuts up when she sees her husband.

"LOOK INTO MY EYES RIGHT NOW! LOOK!" the man shouts.

The kid steps outside the room, but he doesn't go away. He can still see inside.

The woman does as she's commanded and looks into her husband's eyes. Hers are wide with fear and hate. Hate for being made to do this since it isn't the first time. It was not even the hundredth. This is where the watching and the obsession with eyes stem from. One of the places, anyway. This man and this woman and the kid's need to watch it all.

"LOOK IN MY EYES AND TELL ME YOU'RE NOT FUCKING HIM!" the man screams, spittle striking the woman's face. She doesn't avert her eyes, though. Doesn't even blink.

"I'm not."

The words are strong, and silence falls over the room once they fade.

The man doesn't move but stares into the woman's eyes for a minute, judging what he sees in them.

Finally, he stands up and looks at the kid hiding outside the doorway. He's across the room before his son can blink.

"Look at me." His voice is lower, but the mother's fear resides in the kid as well. "Have you seen your mother hanging around with him?"

"With who?"

The name is garbled, something else Christian can't hear or know. Not yet, anyway.

"No. No, I haven't, Daddy."

The man stares at him as if the truth rests in the kid's eyes. Eventually, the father stands, showing no shame for baring his body in front of his wife and son.

"Get ready," he tells the woman. "And you, go check the traps. You're gonna need to cook your own dinner. I want yesterday's leftovers tomorrow."

The father walks out of the bedroom, leaving the boy to stare at his mother's back again.

Christian's phone started vibrating in his pocket, bringing him back to the restaurant. He shook his head once, gathering his surroundings again, then pulled the phone out and put it to his ear.

"Hey."

"Okay, I'm good now. What's going on?" Tommy asked.

Christian looked behind the bar, seeing both the bartender and what was probably the manager staring back at him.

"Sorry," Christian said to the bartender. "I sometimes talk more than I should."

"You got that right," the bartender said.

"Hold on," he told Tommy. Christian stood and exited the restaurant, letting the door close behind him before he continued. "Liam. That's our guy."

"How do you know?"

"I just do. There aren't any reports of abuse because the household didn't tell anyone what happened. Those farms, do you know how many people are registered on each one?"

"Yeah, I can find out. Why?"

"Liam's an only child. I didn't know earlier if there were multiple kids, but there was only one. Find out how many farms had three people."

"Okay. I'll head into the office now," Tommy said.

The phone line went dead, and Christian stared at it, the intensity inside finally dying some. Exhaustion crept over him, moving up his body as if he had stepped into a pool of it.

"He's keeping the eyes because he thinks truth is inside them," Christian said to himself.

Without really thinking about it, he found Luke's number on his phone. It rang twice before he answered.

"You're up late," Luke said.

"Can you meet Tommy and me at the office?"

"Sure."

CHAPTER TWENTY-TWO

Tommy looked up from his computer screen as the other two walked in. "You got Luke out of bed?"

"It's important," Christian said, walking quickly across the room and sitting on the chair in front of Tommy's desk.

"When our master calls, I come running," Luke said with a smile. He followed a few steps behind Christian and sat down.

"So far, the system is telling me there are fifty-two farms with three people. If we narrow it down to male children, we're looking at twenty-three."

"We'll find him on one of those," Christian said. "We need to start sending agents out tomorrow, looking at newer residences for both the kids and the parents."

"Okay," Tommy said. "Now tell us what's going on."

Christian nodded and looked down at Tommy's desk. He was tired, running on fumes as opposed to gas.

"He was abused both physically and mentally. I think his

father ruled the household and had a thing about looking into people's eyes. He bought into the belief that they are the windows to the soul, and that's crossed over to our killer."

"So," Luke said, "he's keeping the eyes because he thinks he possesses their souls?"

"I don't think that's exactly it, but it's close."

"Then why are they blue?" Luke asked.

"If I had to guess, I'd say it's because either his mother or father's eyes were blue." Christian looked up at Tommy. "Actually, can you narrow the search down for houses where the mother or father had blue eyes?"

"If they had driver's licenses, I should be able to, but I'm going to need more time for that. We'll still start sending people out tomorrow morning. How sure are you that we'll find him this way? I'm only asking because we're going to have to use a lot of resources on this, and if you're wrong..."

"My career is over. I know," Christian said. "I'm sure."

"Listen," Luke said. "While we're all here, I want to bring up something that's a bit on the fringes of this case, but you might hear of it. I want to get it in the open before she reaches out to you. Or, again, in Tommy's case. You know Veronica Lopez, right?"

Tommy nodded. He remembered sending her to John Presley. The now deceased John Presley. "Woah. You don't think she has something to do with this, do you?"

"No, no," Luke said. "But, when she went to speak to Presley, he told her the story that I was poisoning him, and that's why he killed the thief. His death has her sort of paranoid, and I'm not sure if she's going to try to make something out of it. I just wanted you to know, in case she keeps asking questions."

"She came to me," Christian said. Tommy looked at the kid, but he kept his eyes on the floor.

"What did she say?" Luke asked.

"What you basically said. She thinks something about the death was abnormal. Thinks you had something to do with it."

"Did you say anything?" Tommy asked.

"I told her that if she had any evidence to let me know." Christian didn't look up, and Tommy glanced at Luke.

"That's good," Luke said. "It won't be a big deal, but I just wanted you all to know. Now, Tommy, what do you want me to do about getting agents to these houses?"

***

Luke drove home an hour later. It was nearing two in the morning, but he felt none of the exhaustion the other two were experiencing. Luke was alive, nearly crackling with energy. He kept his outward demeanor calm like always, but inside, his mind was ablaze with possibilities.

Christian Windsor had lied to the two of them. He hadn't simply said, "Bring me evidence," or at least, Luke didn't think that was what he meant, even if he had said those words.

Dr. Windsor thought Luke might have had something to do with old John's death. The question that mattered was why? What had given him that idea when it had occurred to no one else?

That was why Waverly brought him on board, though.

He could see things others couldn't, not even Luke. Somehow, Christian sensed Luke's true nature.

An approaching car's lights shone on Luke, revealing the grin on his face. The lights faded, and he went back to sitting in darkness.

Perhaps Christian didn't sense his *true* nature. No, that would be too frightening for the boy to handle. He sensed something wasn't right, however, and how far would he follow it? Or would he focus on what the FBI told him to focus on? Was he a rule follower or a contrarian? Luke thought someone like Christian would find it easier to follow rules. Less confrontation.

It didn't matter.

The gates to Luke's driveway opened, and he pulled the car into his garage. He didn't go directly inside the house but walked around the back of the car and out to the front yard. He listened to the night's version of silence, with insects filling some of the void left by the lack of automobiles.

"How far do you want to take this, Mr. Windsor?" Luke said aloud. "How far do you want to follow your inclination that something might not be completely right with me?" He paused for a few minutes, breathing in the smell of his freshly cut lawn. "I hope not too far because I'm enjoying getting to know you. Just give it a little time, and then we can follow that inclination as far as you'd like."

Luke turned from the front yard and went inside the house. He needed to text his new friend and better understand what exactly was happening on that front. Once on his couch, Luke pulled out the cellphone and typed in a text message.

Did you see her?

Yes.

What do you think?

Are her eyes blue? I couldn't see them.

Luke smiled. Ms. Lopez had been wearing sunglasses, but that wasn't what amused Luke. Mr. Windsor had been right. The boy was after his mother's eyes. Luke was certain that if he asked and convinced his friend to talk about it, that would be the answer.

They're brown. Use it for misdirection.

Radio silence for a few minutes as Luke's friend thought about the text. Silence on *Luke's* end as well, but he knew the other side was full of thoughts, that if heard, would rouse an entire neighborhood. His friend was on the verge of losing whatever cool he possessed. The psychology of psychopathy was close to that of addiction, the intensity increasing with each murder.

Okay. She'll be different, though.

How so?

I'm leaving them alive from now on to separate myself from the idiot who killed the FBI agent.

Oh, this was getting too good. Luke's smile widened. Ms. Lopez would have a long life, it looked like, but one where she walked in darkness instead of light. Luke wondered if she could type without looking at her keyboard. He would hate to slow down the writing of her book.

And what of Christian Windsor? Wouldn't Lopez's death push him further toward his inclinations? Yes, most likely. Maybe Luke had been wrong outside. Maybe the time was right for Christian to recognize what so many others couldn't.

CHAPTER TWENTY-THREE

The sun was going to rest below the horizon. At least it was from Veronica's view, but in reality, the sun never rested. Veronica could relate to that since she had been running herself ragged for the past three days. She'd slept six hours total, two each night, and if she didn't rest soon, she thought she might collapse.

She was following too many things at once, yet she didn't have much choice.

On the Friday of her abduction, Veronica Lopez had drunk six cups of coffee by noon and was walking into an interview with Professor George Nintz.

She had spoken to him on the phone a few days earlier, and he had been willing to do the whole interview over the phone, but Veronica didn't want to. She needed to be face-to-face when she asked these questions about Luke Titan. She wanted to see what people *looked* like when they answered. She needed the details, the tiny facial movements—things that even visual conversations on the computer couldn't transfer.

She'd flown to Boston and now sat outside the professor's office. The door was cracked open, and it sounded like he had a student with him.

Veronica was ready this time, her questions prepared and her strategy on point.

The student walked out of the office, and a few seconds later, Dr. George Nintz walked out as well. He stopped in front of Veronica's bench.

"Ms. Lopez?" The professor extended his hand.

"Oh, please call me Veronica." She stood and shook his hand.

"As long as you call me George."

"Sure," Veronica said, smiling.

"Well, come on in, and we can get started."

Veronica followed the professor inside his office and sat down.

"So, you want to talk about Luke Titan, right?"

"Yes."

"And you mentioned on the phone that this isn't strictly dealing with the Sphere?" George asked.

"Yes, that's correct as well. I will say, though, that I'd like for you to speak as an anonymous source if you're okay with that. I'd rather not go public with your name if I do publish this."

"Why?"

Veronica needed to walk *this* tightrope carefully because no net waited for her if she fell. She had to make the man understand the safety concerns without actually voicing them aloud. She couldn't come out and say, "Because if Luke Titan knows you spoke to me, you might end up dead." That wouldn't be great for this man's lifespan or her career.

"The things I'm going to ask you about are very sensitive. If I publish any of this, and I'll let you know before I do, it could create problems for people's careers. If you're anonymous, then those problems are less likely to arise."

The professor leaned back in his chair and crossed one leg over the other. He was quiet for a few moments, then said, "What would you like to talk about, Veronica?"

"You were friends with Trevor Rollins, weren't you?"

George nodded.

"How close were the two of you?" Veronica didn't turn on her phone's recorder. She wanted to hear what the man had to say, and she didn't want him spooked by the recording. If something came of this, she could record another interview later.

"I suppose he was my best friend. We collaborated on quite a few projects. Our families vacationed together. We smoked a lot of cigarettes outside that front door while talking about work, long after everyone else had gone home."

"In that case, I'm sorry for your loss, Doctor. I mean, George."

"Thank you," he said, and he looked genuine in his appreciation.

"You're welcome. I'm going to be blunt with my questions because I don't know any other way to be. Do you think Doctor Rollins killed himself?"

The professor was older than Veronica by perhaps twenty years. He was fit, and his body not carrying much fat. His eyes were a deep brown, and he moved them from

Veronica to the office window when she asked the question.

Thirty seconds passed in silence. Veronica wanted to say something to move the conversation along, but she knew better than to do that. He would answer or he wouldn't, but she couldn't force it.

"How else would he have died?" the professor asked, relieving Veronica's tension.

"I would say either he committed suicide, or he was murdered."

George nodded and kept looking out the window. "I suppose. I'll be honest with you. I thought about this a lot when it happened. Trevor wasn't depressed. He'd only been appointed dean a few years earlier, and he was doing a great job. He loved his wife, and she loved him. He loved his kids."

"Then why would he do it?"

George shook his head. "I don't know. The coroner said it was suicide, though. Trevor had a closed casket funeral." His eyes were still hard, but his voice was just above a whisper. "We talked *a lot*, and I would never have thought it possible."

"What was happening between him and Luke Titan?"

With that, George's eyes flashed back to Veronica. "What?"

"There was some kind of political struggle between the two, right?"

"Yeess," George replied, stretching the word out.

"What was happening? So far, I've gathered that Dr. Rollins was criticizing Titan for spending too much time focusing on other projects and spreading himself too thin. Is that true?"

George's chuckle had spite layered throughout it. "That's part of it, yes. Luke had pretty much abandoned the grants he'd been given, throwing entire research projects onto graduate assistants. He missed class. Trevor told me once that Luke had missed more classes than he had shown up for. Tenure only goes so far, Veronica. He had abandoned his job."

"Was that all of it?"

"No, of course not. There was real animosity there, and it extended beyond the professional."

"Will you tell me about it?"

George sighed. He looked back out the window. "Why are you bringing this up? What good is going to come out of dredging up all this past history? Trevor is dead, and Luke is gone. Working for the FBI, I believe. Talking about this won't bring Trevor back, and if you're hinting that Luke might have had something to do with his death? Well, good luck proving that."

"Another person who criticized Luke Titan died," Veronica said. "And not well."

George closed his eyes and brought his fingers to the bridge of his nose. He scooted his chair under the desk and placed both elbows on it.

"Will you tell me about it?"

Bradley understood that luck affected everyone's life. *It was the great equalizer, not guns.* Sometimes it shone on you, and sometimes it didn't. Sometimes its brother Bad Luck showed up and scorched you.

Bradley knew the brother well. He'd met him early in life, and the bastard had stuck around for a long time. It only made sense that the bright side of the kinship would show up now. Bradley deserved it, and if his Good Luck was someone else's Bad Luck, so what? If it was a zero-sum game, Bradley had lost enough to deserve some wins.

He requested two days off from work, thinking that would be enough time to do everything he needed. Bradley had an idea of how he wanted it to go, with the end being the most important. He envisioned the woman walking down the street, blind—and bandaged, because Bradley wasn't cruel like his father—holding her hands out in front of her while blood leaked from her eye sockets to her cheeks, before finally running down her neck.

He hadn't decided if he would leave her naked when he freed her or whether she should wear clothes, but that was ancillary. Watching her stumble forward, hands in front, desperately trying to find help while cars drove past her, the drivers staring but too frightened to do anything. That was what he wanted. That was what he would have.

He waited until Lopez left for work, though when he saw her get into a cab, he wondered if that would mess up his plans. She wasn't carrying any luggage, only a messenger bag and a purse. Neither indicated she was taking a long trip.

He decided he'd try anyway. If she didn't show up by tomorrow morning, then he'd go home and tell whoever was texting him to fuck off. He didn't have time for mess-ups. Didn't have room for them, and given the frequency of his headaches, he knew that he needed to do something quickly.

He went around to the back of the house, careful to keep an eye out for anyone who might see him. Everything looked clear. He found the door he wanted easily enough and pulled a long dish towel from his back pocket. He wrapped it around his elbow—he'd worn a long-sleeve shirt for extra protection—and then hit the door's glass window.

It shattered and fell to the floor, causing Bradley to jump back. He looked around the backyard, but there was nothing to see. Nothing to hear, either. Not even dogs barking.

He reached carefully through the door and turned the lock on the other side. He needed to be quick because he had to check if there was an alarm. He rushed to the front hallway, searching, but he was not able to find the small box.

"*GODDAMMIT!*" he shouted, panic rising in him. If it went off, he was fucked. *Fucked.* He quickly turned left, then right, and found the keypad.

He read the word on the screen: **INACTIVE**.

Good luck after all. Veronica Lopez's alarm system wasn't armed. Bradley didn't know why and didn't care. Had she armed it, he would have had to figure out another way to take her or abandon the idea. Luck had made neither of those options necessary, though.

Bradley let out a long sigh, and at the end of it, he dropped his backpack on the floor. He had brought everything he needed to take the woman, and if he couldn't take her, he had the tools for that as well.

Bradley took his time walking around the house, looking at pictures and checking the medicine cabinets. He liked to watch. He had loved watching Crystal at the bar, and once he'd found out where Lauren York lived, he'd watched her for weeks, too. Bradley couldn't watch Veronica, but he could see a large part of her life.

That would do until she got home.

Veronica couldn't process what George Nintz told her without sleep. She thanked the professor and said she'd be in touch with him soon. She meant it, too. There was something beneath the surface, and it all swirled around Luke Titan. She knew *that* with an unshakeable certainty, and George Nintz knew it too. He might have known it for some time, even if he never said a word to anyone.

How could he?

Who would believe him?

Who had believed John Presley?

No one.

Veronica didn't even pull her computer out when she got on the plane. She simply leaned her seat back as soon as they allowed it and closed her eyes. Sleep came soon after, and in it, she dreamed. She stood fifty feet away from Luke Titan on an empty street. The sun was coming up behind him, and his shadow cast long on the road. Buildings lined it, so there was only forward or backward for Veronica. She could run away or walk down the road to meet the menace before her. Despite the sun behind him, she saw him smiling. His teeth were white amid the shadows around him. He was smiling at her, daring her to come and challenge him as others had.

The landing jolted Veronica awake.

She grabbed the armrests, sucking in a quick breath before realizing what was happening. Luke Titan wasn't in front of her, just another airplane seat.

It was a dream. You're home, she thought.

Veronica exited the plane. She'd only brought her computer bag and purse, so she skipped Baggage Claim and went to the cab rank.

She hailed one quickly and told the driver her address.

When she made it into her house, she dropped everything on the kitchen table and went to bed. She didn't bother taking her clothes off. Veronica's sleep was deep and dreamless.

Bradley stood above the woman, her head no more than eighteen inches from his leg.

He wore latex gloves and stretched pantyhose around his face. He had it pulled up above his eyes at the moment so that he could truly see her.

He heard her walk into the house. He had been drowsing under one of the guest beds upstairs. She hadn't done much, just put her things down and gone to bed. Bradley let himself wake a bit more, then he pulled himself out from under the bed. He was wearing everything he needed, and he had shaved his body as well as his head. The FBI wouldn't find any evidence from him here.

When he looked at Lopez, he thought she was the most

beautiful of the three he'd taken so far. She was in her mid-thirties, but her dark Latina skin looked smooth in the barely lit bedroom.

Bradley bent down so his ear was next to her mouth. Her breath breezed lightly across his face. He turned so that his lips almost touched her and looked at her closed eyelids.

"What color are they?" he asked, his words barely escaping.

She didn't stir.

He brought both hands up, one holding a rag and the other empty. He held the rag next to her face for a second, getting another glimpse at the peace that would soon flee from her, and then plunged it down.

Her eyelids burst open, and her body stiffened as she struggled to throw him off. He pressed down harder, and her fight softened.

And then it ended, her eyes closing again.

He took his hand and opened the right one.

Not blue, but brown. Bradley suddenly understood that was perfectly fine.

CHAPTER TWENTY-FOUR

Luke opened the letter. He felt surprised for the first time in a while, not expecting to receive a handwritten note from anyone. Luke had strong feelings about letter writing, an art form that was nearly lost from the world. He knew there was no use raging against its demise, though email had done more to destroy people's civility than nearly anything else. Email had led to the invention of social media and from there to sending pictures to one another instead of actual thoughts and feelings.

So, receiving a letter early in the morning from someone he didn't know? Well, he liked it.

Luke opened the envelope, careful not to tear it. Respect should be paid to someone who had taken the time to write to him, then fold the letter inside a protective shield, find postage, and get it to the US Postal Service. Luke would show that respect.

He pulled the letter out and read it.

When finished, he looked out his office window, seeing

Christian walking back from the coffee machine. Luke smiled and waved.

"My friend has made an enemy, it appears," he began as Christian came into his cubicle.

Now Luke knew his friend's name: Bradley Brown.

"What do we have?" Christian said as he crossed Tommy's office. "Also, when do *I* get an office? I'm tired of sitting on the floor with the proletariat."

Tommy smiled. "When you start making arrests. Or one arrest."

"You want to bet how many arrests I have at the end of my career?" Christian said. He looked down as he spoke, smiling slightly. "I bet it's more than you."

"Not if your career lasted four hundred years and mine ended tomorrow," Tommy said. "Now quit baiting me, and let's look at this. So far, we've had agents at eleven of the twenty-three ex-farm families. Nothing is showing up yet. We've got one in Atlanta, and that's where you and I are heading right now. The father died eleven years ago, and the farm went up for sale the year after."

Christian looked up. "He's our guy."

"If your farm theory's correct, it would seem like it, but we're not going to get a warrant based on dreams. We have to go to the house and see what we see. They taught you all this at Quantico, right?"

"He's our guy," Christian repeated. "What's his name?"

"Bradley Brown."

At eight in the morning, Luke, Tommy, and Christian arrived at 2242 Briarbrick Lane.

Tommy took the lead, knocking on the door. Christian stood just behind to his left, Luke on the right. Luke found it interesting that all three understood who was killing these people at nearly the exact same time, even if by different means. Of course, there was no such thing as fate, only circumstance. Luke still found it entertaining.

The door opened, and Luke saw his friend for the first time.

A young man, though they all knew his age from the files they had read earlier that morning. He was twenty-eight and his eyes were blue, just like those he took.

"Can I help you?" the man asked.

"We're looking for a Bradley Brown," Tommy said.

"That's me."

"I'm Special Agent Thomas Phillips. To my right is Special Agent Luke Titan, and on my left is Agent Christian Windsor. We want to speak to you for a few minutes."

To the man's credit, he showed no nervousness.

"What's this about?"

"A case we're working on. We are moving through leads and your name came up, so we thought you might be able to help us."

Bradley smiled. "I'm all for helping law enforcement. Come on in. I do have to be at work in two hours, so hopefully, this won't take too long." Bradley opened the door wider and motioned the agents to move inside.

"Thank you," Tommy said.

Luke understood why Bradley invited them in. It had nothing to do with not looking guilty and certainly nothing to do with helping. Bradley thought he was smarter than the three of them. He would prove it right now by answering all their questions and giving them nothing usable. He'd send them off, and when he was finished, he'd go back to work on Veronica Lopez.

At least, Luke hoped he was working on her.

There was also the pesky letter to deal with. Mr. Brown had a lot on his plate, even if he didn't know it yet. Luke was happy to spoon-feed him, however.

The four men stood in the living room, and Bradley asked them to sit down.

"So, what can I help with?"

"You grew up on a farm, correct?" Tommy asked.

"Yes. Me, my mother, and my father. Well, Father grew up there. Mother married into it."

"And your father? What happened to him, Mr. Brown?"

"He passed away on the farm. A bad accident."

Luke watched Bradley's face as he spoke, and right on cue, he showed the perfect amount of sadness. He even looked down at his feet, breaking eye contact with Tommy.

You've practiced this, Bradley, Luke thought. *And you know your role well.*

"How long have you lived here, Mr. Brown?"

"Eight or nine years, I think. My mother and I."

"Where is she?" Tommy asked.

"She's asleep."

The first crack in the man's armor. He hadn't expected the question. How long had it been since anyone asked about his mother? Years, probably. She might be asleep, but

Luke thought Mr. Brown didn't want anyone speaking to her, ever.

"Mr. Brown, there are some dates we'd like you to take a look at," Tommy said as he handed a piece of paper over. "You'll see them right there. Is there any way you can account for your whereabouts on those dates?"

"Hey, woah," Bradley said. "I thought you were asking for my help. This sounds like you're accusing me of something."

"No, sir. By telling us where you were on those days, you're helping tremendously."

"I'll have to look at my work schedule. These are a lot of days. I'm sure I was working for some of them. If I wasn't there, I was here."

"With your mother?" Luke asked.

"Yes."

Luke glanced at Christian. The boy wasn't looking at Bradley Brown but rather at the area around him. He was scanning the living room and trying to sneak peeks into the kitchen and back hallway.

"Mr. Brown, would you mind if we looked around?" Tommy said.

"Actually, I *would* mind," Bradley said. "I think I'd like you three to leave. I can account for my whereabouts, but it's better that you speak to my lawyer about all this. I'll have him contact you."

Tommy looked at Luke and gave an almost impercep-tible nod. He knew. Christian knew. Luke knew too, but not in the same way.

"Certainly. We might be following up with a warrant to search the premises, and we need you to confirm your whereabouts by tomorrow evening." Tommy stood up from the couch.

"Sure," Bradley agreed.

Luke thought his friend might not be feeling quite as smart at that moment.

"What do you think?" Tommy asked.

"It's him," Christian stated.

"Yup," Tommy agreed. "Luke?"

Christian watched Luke nod, then looked out the car window. "I agree. I think we've got him. Now we just have to prove it."

"The eyes are in his house somewhere," Christian continued.

"Most likely, yes, but we've got to figure out how to get in there. No judge is going to give us a warrant yet." Tommy started the car and pulled out of the driveway. "We'll need a tail on him starting today. Either of you two want the duty until we can have agents assigned to it?"

"I'll take it," Luke said.

"Not going to pawn it off on the newbie?" Tommy asked.

"He needs sleep. You can look at him and see that."

Christian was grateful for the respite. He hadn't slept last night. Dreams were beginning to plague him in a way they never had before. Bad dreams. Frightening dreams.

"All right, let's head back to the office. Luke, you'll need to get a car and head back out here until we can assign a relief team."

"I know, Dad," Luke said.

Christian leaned back against the headrest and quit actively listening to their conversation. He closed his eyes and thought back to Bradley Brown's house. Everything had been in perfect order. A bachelor living with his mother? That might have made sense, yet it didn't *feel* like he lived with her. It felt like she lived with him. That would make the cleanliness more suspect.

What does that matter? Christian wondered. *He can't be clean? You're clean. Does that mean you kill people?*

Of course not, but everything seemed too ordered. Too perfect.

Except when Tommy asked about his mother. That hadn't been ordered. That definitely hadn't fit into Bradley Brown's neat little life.

Christian felt like he should go into his mansion. Another movie was ready to play, one about Brown's father. Something happened on the farm, though perhaps not an accident. Christian was too tired to watch it. He didn't want to see any more gore right now.

"Luke, what did the file say happened to Brown's father?" Christian asked with his eyes still closed.

"Farm accident. Apparently, a tractor started running while Mr. Brown was in front of it. The tractor cut him down right quick, as they might say on a farm."

Christian nodded. "Gruesome and brutal."

"That fits our suspect, though. Mrs. Presley's death was nothing if not gruesome and brutal."

Christian felt Veronica Lopez's questions rise in his mind at the mention of the Presleys. He shoved them away hard.

"The key is his mother," Christian stated. "We've got to get in touch with her."

"If she's alive. By the way, I got an email while we were inside. An old ID. Her eyes are blue," Tommy told them.

"The question is," Luke said, "whether he's taking blue eyes in tribute or retribution."

"I'm betting retribution," Tommy replied.

"Sometimes," Luke mused, "we hurt those we love the most. Maybe Mr. Brown hurts those people because he cares about his mother."

"It doesn't fucking matter. He can tell it to his court-appointed psychiatrist after we catch him."

Christian kept quiet for the rest of the trip, wishing he could nap but knowing what waited for him if he did.

CHAPTER TWENTY-FIVE

Luke didn't follow Bradley to work. The unmarked car he was using had GPS installed in it, so if someone wanted to keep an eye on Luke, they could. He didn't care, though. If anyone asked, he would simply say Bradley Brown hadn't left his house.

Luke wasn't sure how he would use this to his advantage yet, but he wanted to check up on Veronica Lopez, the reporter who couldn't quit chasing after him. Luke knew she had been up to Harvard, though not who she spoke to. Hacking into her computer records hadn't been hard, and when he saw the round-trip ticket to Boston, he understood where she was going.

She knew about Trevor. Someone else who couldn't leave well enough alone. Luke was glad that people like Trevor and Veronica existed. They made Luke's purpose that much easier to accomplish. They sniffed around areas they shouldn't. Perhaps they were agents of God, just as Luke was something else's agent.

He waited until Bradley left, then walked up to the

front door. He didn't bother looking around since he didn't care who saw him. After all, Zeus didn't come down from Mount Olympus to argue with farmers about the weather.

It only took him a moment to open the front door. He picked the deadbolt with ease. Mr. Brown should invest in better security if he was going to run a torture chamber inside his house.

Luke closed the door behind him and stood in the stillness for a moment. He had been able to smell the other two people inside Mr. Brown's house when they had entered that morning. One smelled older, the odor of ashy skin and regret. The other? Fear. That was Ms. Lopez, and Luke wanted to check on her.

He hoped Bradley had started. If not, Luke would have to push him harder. He couldn't hold off the investigation forever, and he wanted the nasty business to be over before they raided the house.

Luke walked to the back bedroom, following the scent of fear to the correct door. He opened it, and Ms. Lopez gave a small scream. Luke peeked in at first, making sure that the woman was blindfolded. Bradley had done a good job with that if nothing else.

Luke stepped inside.

She hadn't been touched yet. Veronica Lopez lay naked on the bed, her arms and legs tied to the bedposts and a black towel tied around the upper half of her face.

Luke didn't even think she'd been raped. Nothing. He was just holding the woman captive. Luke looked around the room quickly, seeing that the window had been boarded from the inside and the rest of the room soundproofed with foam wedges. Mr. Brown had invested a lot of money in this little torture chamber, but he wasn't getting his money's worth because no torturing was occurring.

"Are you here?" Lopez asked.

Luke stepped back and shut the door.

He heard the woman yelling, but only barely. The soundproofing worked well.

Luke walked back down the hall, following the smell of regret. He opened the door and was hit by the room's darkness. The interior smelled sour to him, like something rotting from the inside. Something that should be dead but wasn't.

"Bradley?" a woman lying on the bed asked.

Mr. Brown's mother.

"Bradley, is that you?"

Luke stepped further into the room and closed the door behind him.

"You're not Bradley," the woman stated. She turned her head to look at him, and Luke saw everything he needed. Even in the darkness, the empty holes in her head were readily apparent. Mr. Brown had taken her eyes.

Luke stepped up next to the bed. The woman reached out blindly to feel him but missed by inches.

"Where's Bradley?" she asked.

Luke said nothing, only inhaled the room's stench.

After a few more moments, he left the room, shutting the door behind him. The woman still called Bradley's name, but her voice was faint through the door.

Luke had a few more things to do before he could leave.

Luke walked down the hall to a door on his left. The deadbolt was locked. Mr. Brown had the key, obviously.

"So that's where you keep your trophies," Luke said. He didn't try opening it. Sooner or later, he would see inside.

Luke made his way to Mr. Brown's room. Sitting down at the man's computer, he maneuvered through the weak security and began dropping evidence onto his hard drive. He had to make sure that when Mr. Brown's computer was searched, there would be ample material for Tommy and Christian to understand why John Presley and Veronica Lopez had been harmed. Mr. Brown had to be obsessed with Luke Titan. Not just during Luke's time with the FBI but before as well.

Luke loaded mountains of information onto the hard drive in places Mr. Brown would never think to search but FBI technicians would. He even disguised the date the data was written to the hard drive.

"Okay," Luke said, reverting the computer to its original state.

He stood and left the house, careful to lock the door before going to his car. Now he needed to deal with Charles Ranger.

"I bet you hate being called 'Charlie,' don't you?" he asked, remembering the letter.

What should he do with the old man?

An interesting question, but Luke wasn't quite ready to answer it yet. Alas, he should probably do his due diligence and follow Mr. Brown to his place of work.

Veronica listened to the door shut.

"*HEY!*" she screamed, knowing it was useless.

While lying on this bed, she had screamed until her throat was raw, but nothing had come of it. She wasn't sure if the room was soundproofed or if she was out in the middle of nowhere, but whoever had taken her didn't care if she screamed until she passed out.

Veronica was glad the door was closed, though. Glad that whoever had come in had left. She was cold in the air-conditioned room. She remembered the grubby paws that had undressed her. They had done it quickly, thank God, as if they were embarrassed to be doing it. At first, she had thought she would be raped, so she had whimpered and begged as the clothes came off. Cried out and screamed as her arms and legs were spread to the bed's four corners, sure the sick invasion would take place next.

But it never came.

She had no idea how long she'd been here, but outside of urinating on herself and being naked, not to mention blindfolded, she hadn't been harmed.

That wouldn't last, though. Sooner or later, the man who took her would do what he wanted, and Veronica knew that wouldn't be an oil massage and a kiss on the cheek. If she didn't get out of here, she would be dead—after being raped.

She briefly wondered if Luke Titan had done this to her. She wondered about many things as she lay alone in the dark. This wasn't Luke Titan's style, though. He wasn't one to tie up his victims and keep them around. This was a different kind of psychopath.

That was all Veronica knew. She was in a psychopath's house, and no one had any idea she was missing.

Yes. Yes. Yes.

Charles could barely believe the words coming from the psycho's mouth, but with each new one that spilled out, Charles' happiness grew exponentially.

"Those *motherfuckers*." The word came out in an angry hiss.

Bradley was in front of Charles' bed, pacing. The door to his room was closed so no one could look in on them when he was ranting.

"They think they've got me, I bet. They said they would get a goddamn warrant if they needed it. I'm supposed to get a lawyer! Where the hell am I going to get a lawyer, Charlie?" Bradley stopped walking and looked at the man. "Do you know any?"

Charles shook his head vehemently.

"No, of course not. You're just an old geezer who can't talk. Well, they're not going to catch me. No fucking way. I'll burn the damned house down before I get caught."

Charles watched him pacing, more than shocked that his letter had worked so quickly. He'd sent it…what, two days ago or so? And already the FBI was at the psycho's door, discussing warrants. Charles could have stood up and danced a jig all around the bastard if his legs worked. He would have danced from one end of this nursing home to the other and sang, too.

Instead, he sat there motionless, trying to keep his face from showing the joy he felt.

"I've got to do something quick. I just don't know what.

I don't want to leave. I mean, I'm just getting started. The garage isn't nearly full."

Did this idiot really think he'd be able to fill up his garage-turned-in-to-a-freezer with eyeballs? Had he thought no one would catch him? He could just kill an endless amount of people and then put on a thick jacket and sit down in the middle of his artwork, five hundred eyeballs looking at him?

Yes, Charles supposed that was exactly what he'd thought.

But he's not thinking that now. No, he's worried, and you better start looking out for yourself, old man. He's worried and if he's talking about burning down his house, then you should really consider whether or not he thinks you're a part of that house. Because you're evidence. Just like those eyeballs hanging from his walls.

What Charles needed was to keep the charade going just a bit longer and for the FBI to hurry the hell up with getting into that house.

He waved the madman over to his bed.

"What?" Bradley said, sounding like a fat child who just had candy taken from him.

Charles started writing on his tablet.

Don't burn house. Just hide it.

"Hide it? The fucking house?" Bradley asked.

Jesus Christ, this guy was an idiot.

No. Hide evidence.

"Great idea, Charlie. Where would I hide it?" Sarcasm was thick in the bastard's voice. "Maybe I could turn the common room into the freezer and pin the eyeballs up there? Do you think management would think of it as decoration or as arts and crafts?"

It was hard for Charles not to spit in the psycho's face. Just hock up a huge glob of phlegm, then watch it roll down the bastard's face.

He kept looking at his tablet and moving his pen.

Here. Put it all in a cooler. Keep it under my bed and I'll tell management children brought it. Left it to keep my Cokes cold. No one will look inside.

Bradley took a step back from the bed, his eyes moving to the headboard. Charles wasn't sure what he was doing, only that he had to keep the psycho from burning down the house. *But,* if he brought the eyeballs here, everything was over. Charles *would* talk then. Someone in this place would look at the cooler full of eyeballs under his bed, and then he'd explain in great detail what the fucking psycho had been doing.

Plus, the FBI had the letter. They'd back him up, too.

"That might work, Charlie, if I can trust you with them. It won't be for long, just enough time to let the bastards search the house and find nothing. I'll need to move my computer, but I can find somewhere for that to go. Okay, I'll let them come search the house. They'll see that I've turned my garage into a freezer, but what the hell does that matter?

"I'll need to figure out what to do about Mother, but

again, that's not a deal-breaker. They don't have to meet her." He paused but still didn't look at Charles, just rambled. "This might work." Finally, he glanced at the old man. "If I can trust you. I can, right, Charlie?"

Charles nodded as vehemently as he'd shaken his head earlier.

It didn't occur to Charles until later, when it was too late, why the FBI hadn't come to question him.

<hr>

Luke was staring at his cellphone when the gate's buzzer went off.

He'd been contemplating what to say to Mr. Brown, knowing that the next few messages needed to set him off. Charles Ranger had to die; that was clear. Luke thought that if he could knock off Mr. Ranger and Ms. Lopez just before the cavalry showed up, that would work fine.

The buzzer brought him out of his thoughts. He'd been lost in them, seeing very little of the world around him. He stood from the couch and walked to the intercom, looking out the living room's front windows as he did.

"What time is it?" he asked, his voice taking on the sleepiness. The intercom's camera showed a cab with Christian Windsor sitting in the backseat. The cab had pulled up, and Christian was leaning out his window to speak.

"It's two in the morning. I can't sleep. I called, but your phone's off."

"So, you just decided to show up?"

"I have a problem," Christian said. "You know that."

"You have a lot of problems, Christian. Come on in."

Luke buzzed the cab through and then moved to his bedroom. He quickly shed the clothes he was wearing into a laundry hamper and put a robe on. He looked briefly in the mirror, ran a hand through his hair, and went to answer the door.

"You should invest in Ambien," Luke said as he let Christian in.

"Probably. I don't like taking chemicals, though. I hate the chemicals in the bread I eat, but what can I do?"

"You're wired. You sure you haven't ingested any chemicals tonight?"

"I haven't." Christian walked past Luke into the living room. He didn't sit down but paced in front of the coffee table. "The judge came back. No go on the warrant."

Luke knew already, his phone having notified him when the email arrived. His phone wasn't off. He'd sent Christian to voicemail the two times he'd called.

"Okay," Luke said. "Sit down. Let's talk about it."

"I can't sit. This is the guy, Luke. He's the one, and we have to find a way in."

Luke moved across his living room to his kitchen. "I'm going to make coffee, though I'd advise you don't drink any."

"I don't like chemicals," Christian repeated as he paced.

"This is your first case. It's normal to be this excited, but you have to realize that these things happen. Due process is in place for a good reason, and we can't break it. Better a thousand guilty men go free than one innocent man face the gallows. The saying is true."

He ground up the beans and poured them into the filter.

"Veronica Lopez's agent called me," Christian remarked.

Luke's hand froze as he took in the information. He needed to show surprise. It wouldn't do to keep making coffee.

He turned around. "About what?"

"She can't find Lopez. She's called her for the past two days and gotten nothing. Lopez told her she'd spoken to me, so the agent called me after all her friends and family."

"Veronica Lopez is missing?" Luke asked.

Christian nodded, not looking at the kitchen as he kept pacing across the living room.

"Well, she has to report that to the local police. That's not within our purview, and we certainly don't have time to chase down a reporter right now."

"I know. That's what I told her. It's just... It's on my mind. Look, we have to figure out how to get into the man's house."

Luke turned around and started making the coffee again. "Give me a minute, please." When the coffee was finished brewing, he poured a cup and walked over to the couch. "Sit with me, Christian."

He stopped pacing and looked at the empty spot on the couch but didn't move toward it.

"Pacing will not get us a warrant any faster. It'll only wear my carpet thin. Sit."

Christian listened, sitting on the opposite end from Luke.

"We have twenty-four-hour surveillance on Bradley Brown. Tommy has someone filling in right now, and he's going to take the morning shift. I'll go on tomorrow, and then the fill-in comes again. We took care of the security detail so *you* could get some sleep. You're not, though, and I think it's driving you a bit mad."

Christian stared at the coffee table, his right leg shaking up and down like a miniature jackhammer.

"Why can't you sleep?" Luke asked.

A few seconds passed before Christian answered, "I'm having nightmares."

"Have you had them before?"

Christian shook his head.

"Why do you think they're happening?"

"Are you psychoanalyzing me?"

"No more than you do me when we talk. We're both doctors, even if I'm an M.D."

"And a Ph.D.," Christian added.

"True. What are you seeing in your nightmares?"

"Bradley Brown. He's standing in a room made of mirrors, and it's dark, but there's an infinite number of eyeballs staring out of the mirrors. They glow blue, and they blink. He's grinning like it's all he's ever wanted."

"The dreams scare you?"

Christian nodded.

"Why?"

"Because when the lights come on, the room isn't made of mirrors. It's his mother, and the eyes are hers. She's smiling just like he is. They're both...happy."

Luke didn't say anything for a few seconds. He leaned back in his seat and took a sip from his coffee, placing his feet on the table. He stared out the large front window in front of him.

"Is it his happiness that scares you?" he said. "Bradley Brown's?"

"Yes."

"Because you understand what he's wanting, and you're going to end it."

Christian nodded, though he said nothing.

"What is it he wants?"

"His mother's love."

"And he finds it through the eyes he takes?" Luke said, still not looking at the other agent.

"He's trying to, even if he doesn't know it."

"The first of your doctorates, the one in psychology? You deal with theories of the mind. My medical doctorate deals with matters of the brain. You see into people. What do I see?"

"You see through them, Luke. They don't exist to you."

Luke nodded. "Fairly accurate. Bradley Brown is trying to find order in this world, Christian. He's trying to find security. However, the only way the rest of the world can maintain order is if we throw his world into chaos. You can't let your ability to see him cloud what you have to do to him."

"I know," Christian agreed.

"He's going to slip up soon. When he does, we'll catch him before he kills anyone else."

"You really think so?"

Luke nodded. "I think your dreams will stop, too. Until our next criminal comes along."

CHAPTER TWENTY-SIX

Christian finally left, and Luke was alone again.

The police would begin looking for Veronica Lopez soon, and Luke would make sure they found her. An eyeless reporter who needed to use her ears rather than her eyes for investigative journalism. She would most likely need a braille keyboard, as well.

Luke watched Christian's cab pull out of the driveway. The boy was too afraid to drive, and although he hadn't said it, Luke knew he enjoyed being a passenger since it gave him time to think. Luke just hoped the cab driver would keep silent so he could.

When Christian looked at him, did he see himself, or at least part of himself as Luke did? He couldn't deny it. Wouldn't. Luke lived in reality, and while he wouldn't call himself a Buddhist—and knew no Arhat would ever consider him a Buddhist—he understood the tenets and felt he'd mastered what the Buddha had wanted to teach. To be okay with reality. To not crave or find displeasure with anything.

Perhaps not mastery, but close to it.

Thus, seeing himself in Christian was something he hadn't experienced before. An intelligence that rivaled his own, and perhaps, what Luke might have been if he'd found a different purpose, a different master, earlier.

"What's your purpose, Christian?" he asked the empty living room.

Eventually, Luke knew, Christian would see the truth about him. All Luke's cunning and agility wouldn't be able to keep that mind at bay forever. When he did discover Luke's nature...

"What will I do to you?"

Luke turned from the window as the cab's lights disappeared down the road.

It was time to act. He knew Bradley Brown would soon overreach himself, even if he thought he still controlled the situation. Luke needed to put a bow on everything by then.

He went to his cellphone and typed a message.

Charles Ranger has told the FBI.

Two minutes passed, and he got an answer.

Who is that?

Luke closed his eyes and smiled, picturing Bradley Brown in his room, his computer the only light across the darkness. He saw Bradley's leg shaking up and down, his brow contorted so hard that it hurt but still trying to play games. Trying to make Luke think Bradley needed no one.

He opened his eyes and typed another message.

Have I lied yet? Why do you think they came to your house today? They will be going to talk to Ranger soon.

Another minute passed.

Thx.

Luke put his phone down. He would rest now. Tomorrow, the world would blaze with flame, and he planned to enjoy the show.

The next day, Christian asked that the alternate team be removed from the rotation, and he take over tailing Bradley Brown.

"You're sure?"

He was. He felt a need to be close to Bradley and understand him, as sad as the man was. He wasn't sure if Bradley Brown would die before they could arrest him as Luke had suggested or if he'd spend the rest of his life behind bars. Other options existed, of course, but in the end, Christian wanted to stop him.

To bring chaos to the order he so desperately wants.

Luke's words had stuck with Christian. When he went home from Luke's, he slept soundly. No dreams. No nightmares. No Bradley Brown. Christian always said what he felt, but Luke had the ability to say what was *needed.*

Christian wanted to be near Bradley for his last few hours of freedom or life, whichever he chose.

"We'll do our shifts together, then," Tommy had said in

response to Christian's suggestion. "You're not ready to tail someone on your own. You come and sit through mine. Sleep if you want, and then I'll stay for yours. That work?"

It worked for Christian.

They both sat in the unmarked FBI car. They were in the condominium complex across from Brown's nursing home. The sun had set an hour ago.

"How bored is he in there?" Tommy asked. "Geriatrics go to sleep around four PM, and he has to stay up all night. I might lose my mind too, with nothing to do all night."

"I don't think he's bored now," Christian said. "I think his mind is probably whirling."

"About what?"

"About who he's going to kill next."

"You don't think he's worried about us?" Tommy said.

"Some, but I think he's got a fever, and it's not going to break until he kills. That's what's driving him right now."

Christian was fine with the silence that came in a stake-out. It seemed Tommy was as well. The car remained quiet for most of the stakeout.

"Here he comes," Tommy said.

Christian saw him, too. He was walking out the front door and appeared to be heading for his car.

"His shift can't be over. It's only been a few hours," Tommy remarked.

Christian was quiet. He didn't feel easy about this. A lot of pieces were whizzing around in his head as if a tornado had grabbed the logical machine that normally ran every-thing with such precision. He couldn't put the pieces in place yet, but he could see them all flinging around rapidly. Bradley Brown. John Presley. Luke Titan. Veronica Lopez.

The only person missing was Tommy. He seemed to be the granite that the team was built on. Luke was too...aloof, non-caring.

Yet, that wasn't it, but Christian couldn't figure out what *it* was.

And now he watched Bradley Brown open his trunk and pull something out. Both Tommy and he put binoculars to their eyes.

"It's a cooler," Tommy said.

Christian nodded, the larger vision of Bradley moving up and down in his binoculars. "What's in it?"

"Lunch?" Tommy asked. "I wonder what our killer eats on his night shift."

"That's the first thing anyone's ever said that's made me not have an appetite. Thanks."

"Someone has to look after your weight, my friend."

Bradley had thought all day about how he'd handle Charlie. He knew he had to figure out who was on the other end of the text messages, but that could wait. First Charlie, then the rest.

And the eyeballs. Bradley needed to take care of them as well.

He had thought from the early hours of the morning to the early hours of the afternoon, and only one answer seemed to solve all his problems. If Charlie tipped off the FBI, and they knew where he lived, then Bradley needed to disappear. He didn't know for how long—a few years, probably. Canada was the most likely spot, and as long as he crossed the border before a warrant was placed on him, he'd be fine. Maybe he could start again up there, or maybe he'd come back to the States.

Mother needed to die. It would be sad, but it was necessary.

Most killers, Bradley knew, couldn't stop. They were compelled to keep going. Bradley now understood why, but he had two more people left to kill before he could make his break for freedom. Two more should stave off the headaches for a time. Two more should give him some space.

At least he hoped that. This was new territory for him.

He did as Charlie had said and carefully bagged up his eyeballs, then placed them in the small cooler. Before leaving his house, he walked it out to the trunk, packed full of ice, and set it inside.

He wouldn't leave the eyeballs with Charlie, of course. No, now that Charlie had betrayed him, he wanted the old man to see what was going to happen to him. Except Charlie and the bitch back at his house would both live through it, then walk around eyeless for the rest of their days.

Bradley just wanted to scare the old fuck before he cut him up.

He walked through the front doors and took a right down the hallway toward Charlie's room. He said hello to Sarah as he passed her.

"What's that?" the bitch asked.

"Oh, just putting some ice in Ranger's cooler. You know how he is with his Cokes."

"He's got a cooler for them now?"

"Yeah. His kids brought it for him, and he's obsessed with it."

Sarah smiled and let Bradley move down the hall. He would be glad never to talk to her again. If he had time, he'd cut her up too because she made him stop in the hallway. Bradley's rage grew with each step. He was furious with Charlie, with the FBI, and with Sarah for speaking to him. All he wanted was something simple. Something pure. Something he could have for himself. But no, they wouldn't let him. No one wanted him to have it. They were going to try to take it away, and fuck them for that.

Bradley reached Charlie's room, put the cooler down, and opened the door. He pushed the cooler in with his foot, then shut the door behind him.

Charlie sat on the bed, his tablet open on his lap. The mute fuck, sitting there and listening for months on end, all the while plotting to take away what he knew Bradley cared so much about.

"How are you, Charlie?"

Charlie nodded, and a smile appeared on his face. How long had Bradley fallen for that smile? It had seemed like the old man was happy to be around people he liked. That was a lie.

"That's good." Bradley slowly walked forward, pushing the cooler across the floor. It scraped against the wood. When he reached the bed, he sat down on it, cooler between his feet. "Charlie, I've had a stretch of good luck and bad luck recently. The bad luck is that the FBI is on to me."

Bradley looked at Charlie, and he saw fear on the old man's face. Finally. "Yeah, I know, buddy. That's a pretty big piece of bad luck, isn't it? The good luck, though, is that someone has been helping me. You know what they did for me today?"

Charlie shook his head.

No, you don't know, Bradley thought. *And you don't want to know either, you old fucking piss bucket. But you're about to know it all, and then you'll really wish you hadn't known.*

"They told me, Charlie, that you were the one who told the FBI."

He stared at the old man as all the color drained from Charlie's face. He was as pale as the sheets he lay on top of, so shocked he couldn't even put up a defense.

"It's true, isn't it?" Bradley asked.

Charlie shook his head again, but the attempt was so poor that it looked more like a spasm than a negative.

"Yes, it is. You and I both know it." Bradley looked down to his feet and was silent for a second. "I brought what we spoke about. I don't think it would be in my best interest to leave it here anymore, though. You get why, right?"

Bradley bent and hoisted the small container up onto the bed, roughly moving the old man's legs out of the way. He stood so the cooler was in front of him. "You see, Charlie, no one else knows as much about me as you do. Not even Mother. I told *you* these things because I thought I could trust you, but now I know I can't."

Bradley lost track of the room around him. The cooler grew bigger in his eyes, a large blue bucket full of his most precious possessions. The only possessions that mattered. The rest of the world could burn down as long as he had these eyeballs.

"I have to leave, Charlie. You're making me do it. I have to go somewhere else where the FBI can't find me, and I won't ever be able to come back here. I have to stop doing this for a while, and I don't want to. I *like* doing this, Charlie. *I really fucking like it.*"

He reached forward and took the cooler's top off, not seeing the horror blooming on Charlie's face like some awful rose born in hell's deepest layer. Bradley reached inside and pulled out a plastic sandwich bag with two solid orbs inside it. The bag was fogged and iced over, but Bradley could still see the two eyeballs, one looking at the ceiling, the other at him.

They were huge in his mind, the size of planets. The rest of the room had fallen away, leaving him with his loves. "I'm not going to keep your eyes, Charlie. You don't deserve to be with the rest. I *am* going to cut them out, though, and I'm going to do it while you're alive. You're going to feel every single tendon and nerve being snipped."

Bradley looked away from the bag at Charlie.

"Are you ready to go?"

CHAPTER TWENTY-SEVEN

Luke was in a rental car, sitting in the same apartment complex as Tommy and Christian. The windows were deeply tinted, right at the legal limit, and the car was parked where no streetlights illuminated it. He sat motionless in the front seat, his eyes staring directly at his partners.

He knew what Mr. Brown was doing and that Tommy would stop him if he went ahead with such a foolish plan. He was going to bring Mr. Ranger right outside, shove him in his car, and just drive home as if he wasn't kidnapping a geriatric patient. Tommy wouldn't let that happen, regardless of if he had to break laws to ensure that Mr. Ranger didn't die.

Luke couldn't allow *that* to happen, not yet anyway.

Mr. Brown had walked into the nursing home about an hour ago, carrying his cooler of trophies. Oblivious to the fact that he was being watched. Luke would help, though. Luke would save the day, at least for a little while.

He stepped out of his car and closed the door silently. He didn't bother locking it but simply walked away, moving through the back of the complex and out the exit. He walked swiftly and without a sound, like a predator stalking prey through the night jungle. It took him five minutes to walk around the back of the nursing home, making sure that Tommy and Christian couldn't see him.

He reached the back door and didn't pause, just simply walked in. The world made it easy for predators because they thought that while predators might exist, they were protected. Bad things happened to other people, but not to *them*. Not the real bad things anyway. What they didn't know—and truthfully, most never would—was that predators walked around them every day, ready to snatch them up and take them back to painful lairs.

Luke was the bad things, all of them wrapped into one single body. But that was okay, good even. It took Luke years to understand this, though he didn't ever really fight his nature. There was a God, Luke knew, even if not the one the Jews and Christians prayed to. That God was a thing of goodness, a thing that wanted to keep order in the world. To fight the bad things.

That's not the way the world should work, though, and Luke was intent on doing his part to destroy the order that God so desperately wanted in place. As if He should have complete say over this dominion.

A woman sat at a small desk to the right of the door.

"Hi?" she said. "I'm sorry, sir, but you'll need to go around to the front. But you'll really have to come back tomorrow. Visiting hours are over."

Luke said nothing, just moved as swiftly as he had outside. He reached her desk in seconds, and just as she opened her mouth to say something with quite a bit more alarm than her first few sentences, he snapped her neck. He felt the bones break beneath the strength of his hands.

Her body tried to slump forward, but Luke held her up. He lifted her as easily as a bulldozer lifts dirt, hoisting her over his shoulder and looking around the large room. Luke saw the closet, took her to it, and tossed her body inside. He shut the door, then surveyed the room once more. Everything was in order besides the person missing from her station, which was fine. He'd leave this place long before anyone noticed.

Luke went to the dead woman's computer. The screen was on, and she had logged in. He found the program detailing the residents' rooms and located Mr. Ranger.

He left the room as a shadow would, nothing remaining to show he'd ever been there. Luke walked down the halls with a purposeful stride that would keep anyone from saying a word to him, though he saw no one. He didn't knock when he reached Ranger's room but simply opened the door and stepped inside, closing it behind him.

Mr. Brown stood over Mr. Ranger, a rag lying on the old man's face. Mr. Ranger was unconscious and Mr. Brown in a trance, staring at the geriatric as if the secret to the universe resided within his decrepit body.

Mr. Brown looked at Luke slowly, his brain desperately trying to bring him back to reality.

Luke put his finger to his lips. "Shhh."

"Here he comes," Tommy said.

The hours had rolled by slowly. Tommy and Christian sat in the car, silent for the most part. It was four in the morning, and Bradley Brown's shift was apparently over.

"He's got the cooler," Christian said. "What do we do?"

"What do you think?"

"Follow him?"

"Bingo," Tommy said.

"We just keep following him? That's it? We can't do *anything* else?" Christian said as he turned the key in the ignition.

"That's the definition of a stakeout. We watch until we see something that will let us move on him. This is the majority of detective work, kid. This and paperwork. Very little excitement."

Brown's car left the parking lot, and Christian slowly pulled out of their space. He stayed a good distance back without Tommy needing to say anything.

"I don't like this."

"What?" Tommy asked as they moved onto the highway.

"It doesn't feel right. The whole thing. What was that cooler for?"

"Could be for anything. Could be his lunch. Could be he brought lunch for the staff. Maybe he's a real nice guy outside of his penchant for cutting people's eyes out of their heads."

"No. Something's wrong."

"Maybe, but we can't do anything about it yet."

"I need to think," Christian said, his voice taking on a

tone of worry that Tommy thought bordered on panic. "Look, he's heading home. Can we pull over for just a second and you take the wheel? We'll catch up with him if we're fast."

Tommy looked at his partner. "You're serious?"

"Yes, I'm sorry. I need to think, and I can't do it while driving. It's dangerous."

"I'm starting to wonder about you, Christian. Pull over."

They made the switch quickly, and Tommy roared back onto the highway. He moved down the dark road at just under a hundred miles per hour, his eyes searching for the car he wanted.

"This might look weird," Christian said. "And if you talk to me, I won't answer, but I'm fine."

***

Christian didn't go to the room marked Surgeon.

Instead, he stood in his mansion's foyer. A large staircase split to the right and left in front of him. A painting of his mother hung on the wall at the bottom of the staircase, her kind face surveying Christian's world. It told him everything was okay, and it always would be.

Nothing was okay right now, though, regardless of what the painting said.

Christian couldn't figure out why. He couldn't figure out anything because events were moving too quickly. He had never dealt with anything he couldn't see from all angles at once until now.

Answers were somewhere in this mansion. Christian just needed to figure out where.

He didn't move with his usual speed, trusting Tommy to leave him alone. He walked up the stairs, looking at how sparsely he'd decorated the place over the years. He knew very little about fashion or interior design, but what he had in here was his, and he appreciated it. The stained glass on either side of the staircase showed happy scenes from his life from when he was around his mother or by himself, not facing the outside world. It always seemed far too daunting.

He reached the top of the stairs and peered down the hallway in front of him. He didn't start down it but just stared, understanding that it led to all the rooms his mind had filled.

He knew he'd find a video if he went to the Surgeon's room, but he didn't need to see Bradley Brown kill his father.

"Why am I here?" he asked.

To see what you're missing. Your mind's already seen it. You just haven't brought it up to your consciousness yet.

Christian meandered down the hallway and took a right, then a left. He found himself in front of Luke Titan's room. The writing at the top was in Luke's unique cursive.

Why did you go to this room?

He knew why. Because Veronica Lopez was missing and John Presley was dead. Because Luke had stared at John Presley's body without a single bit of sadness, or humanity. More, he didn't seem to care who saw. That had bothered Christian, though he hadn't put a label to it until this moment.

Christian turned the knob and walked into his mind's record of Luke Titan.

A large painting covered the back wall, painted on the surface. Luke Titan looked back at him, or at least a perfect replica. His brown eyes spoke of intelligence, containing simultaneously both depth and shallowness. The depth said the thoughts that went through his head could hardly be fathomed by others, and the shallowness belied his simplistic view of the world.

Christian turned to the right and saw that the room had expanded, his knowledge of Luke increasing with the time he spent around the man. A large desk sat against the right wall with a thick, large book on top of it. Something new. Christian went to it.

The Life of Luke Titan

He stared at the cover. His mind had never done anything like this before. His insights usually came in the form of live replays, where he stood next to people as they lived through events. Here was something he would need to read, and Christian didn't know how to feel about it.

He opened the book and started reading.

Tommy looked at Christian. His eyes were open, and he stared forward as if he were simply riding in the car, but Tommy knew that wasn't true. Christian had gone somewhere, perhaps to his mansion. Tommy didn't know how he did it or what he was doing in that other place besides "thinking."

"Jesus Christ. I never thought it could get weirder than Luke."

He drove on, having caught up to Brown's car. He stayed forty feet back, the first twinges of fatigue tugging at his body. Hopefully, this would be over soon.

Hopefully, Christian would come back to reality quickly.

CHAPTER TWENTY-EIGHT

"I'm dreadfully sorry about all this, Mr. Ranger."

Luke stood on the patio in Mr. Brown's backyard. Ranger was in front of him, with a blanket draped over his wheelchair to keep the cool night air from bothering him.

Luke opened the back door with the key Mr. Brown had supplied, then he walked over to Mr. Ranger's chair and pushed the elderly gentleman into the house.

"I didn't know you were involved in this until you wrote me. Unfortunately, you chose the wrong agent. My partner, Tommy Phillips, probably would have swarmed all over the letter and made sure Mr. Brown was apprehended *and* you were kept safe. I, on the other hand, deal with things differently."

He stopped the wheelchair just outside the kitchen. The light was on inside, and Luke was glad about that. He didn't mind the dark but he thought Mr. Ranger might, especially in such a strange and foreign place that held many dangers for the old man.

Luke stepped in front of the wheelchair and walked to the kitchen sink, then turned to look at Mr. Ranger.

"Our friend, Mr. Brown, is in a predicament. As are you, I'm afraid. You see, I work for the FBI in a technical sense, but I've found with life that the greatest pleasure comes from serving a higher purpose. Unfortunately for you, the FBI's purpose is not high enough for my needs and is only a means to an end. That end has started just recently."

The old man did nothing, only stared at Luke with an intense mixture of hate and fear.

"I won't lie to you and say you're going to live through this. You won't, but I do promise you're not going to feel the amount of pain that Mr. Brown wants you to. That would be cruel, and you don't deserve that. You're in the wrong place at the wrong time, but take solace, Mr. Ranger. You lived a long, full life and have left behind children who will remember you fondly."

The old man motioned with his hands.

"Paper and pen?"

Mr. Ranger nodded.

"Let me see what I can find." Luke walked down the hall to Mr. Brown's room and saw what he needed. "Here you go."

The old man wrote for a few seconds before turning the pad to Luke.

Fuck you, you fucking psycho. I hope Bradley scrapes your eyes out.

A slow smile spread over Luke's face.

"Oh, you've got some kick in you, don't you, Mr. Ranger?" Lights flashed across the back wall, and Luke looked up. "Speak of the devil and he'll show up. Bradley's home, so let's see whose eyeballs end up getting scraped from their skulls, shall we?"

Bradley was indeed home, and he was not happy. Rage had been replaced by fear and confusion. Bradley still wanted to squish Charlie's fucking eyeballs in his hands, but things were...

Out of control.

He parked the car in his driveway, knowing the FBI was out there watching his every move.

No matter what happened, Bradley always told himself he would be more careful than the people he studied. And somehow, everything he'd planned and hoped for was being dashed. He was quickly seeing there might not be a way out, that he might go down just like every other serial killer.

He still had the cooler, though. He still had his batch of blue eyeballs, and as long as he had them, all wasn't lost.

He knew the man who had shown up in Charlie's room. Bradley had seen him on TV when the FBI announced they were taking over the case. Apparently, this was the man who'd been texting him. Helping him. An FBI agent.

"Jesus. H. Christ," he said, still sitting in the driveway. "What the fuck am I going to do?"

He had listened to the FBI agent's spiel, detailing out that other agents were following him and would continue to until they either had a warrant or Bradley slipped up. The thin agent said they were watching him at that very moment, and if he left with Charlie, he'd be arrested within minutes.

"I still want to help," the agent had said, and Bradley kept listening, mainly because he could find no words of his own.

He ended up giving the FBI agent his house key and agreed to stay for the rest of his shift. What else *could* he do? An FBI agent had caught him dispensing chloroform to an elderly man before telling him his whole world would end if he didn't listen.

Now Bradley sat outside his house, hoping the agent hadn't been bullshitting him and was inside with Charlie.

What are you going to do when you go in there? You two going to drink a few brews and talk about how funny this whole thing is?

Bradley didn't know.

He looked in his rearview mirror to see if he could spot an FBI vehicle, but as the agent had said, he couldn't.

Bradley got out of his car and locked the door, then walked up the driveway and twisted the doorknob. It was unlocked, as the agent had said it would be.

He walked inside.

"We're in here, Mr. Brown," the agent called. Bradley hadn't asked the man's name. He'd been too off balance to say anything at the nursing home.

Bradley walked to the kitchen, where the lithe man was leaning against the kitchen counter. Charlie was bundled up in his wheelchair with a legal pad on his lap.

"Mr. Ranger here was just describing how he wanted you to scrape my eyes out before this was all over. Perhaps you'll have that chance."

"Why are you helping me?" Bradley asked. "And what is your name?"

"Luke Titan," the agent replied. "I'm helping you because, for the time being, your goals and mine intersect."

Bradley stared at the man and thought about what to say next. None of this made sense, but he felt he didn't have any choice. Somehow he'd lost control, and now someone he didn't know stood in his kitchen with all the answers.

"What's your plan?" Bradley asked.

CHAPTER TWENTY-NINE

The Life of Luke Titan

An Introduction

I know his birthdate. I read that on the Internet. I know where he was born, and I know his parents' names, but all that means little.

Because I don't know anything else about him.

But that's not true, is it? I know he looks through people, and I've said it to him. I know that when I watched him stare at John Presley's dead body...and his wife's, he showed no emotion. No anger. No hate. No sadness. Not even a sense that something wrong had been done.

He stared at those bodies like I imagine a psychopath would when his rage is finished, and he's looking at the victim he just raped. The person lying there, writhing in pain, crying, while the psychopath stares as if an ant was crawling on the floor.

This book is in place of a video because I can't see into him. If I wanted to, I could go to Tommy's room in one of my corridors and watch much of his life play out in front of me. Instead of a video, though, my mind has created this collection of thoughts I haven't been able to bring to my consciousness for a multitude of reasons. It is titled The Life of Luke Titan, *but that's a misnomer.*

It should be called, The Lack of Luke Titan's Life *since no one knows a thing about him.*

What else haven't I allowed myself to consider?

I pushed away Veronica Lopez's hypothesis that people who challenged Luke died. Yet, she was challenging him, and now she's missing. I pushed it away, though, because the logic behind it makes no sense, even if my gut tells me something different. He's a world-renowned scientist and doctor and will eventually be known as perhaps the greatest FBI agent ever as well. What reason does he have to murder, or at least create circumstances for people to be killed? His career and life would end if he did that because eventually, he'd be caught. Eventually, everyone is caught.

That's not true either, is it? If Luke is doing these things, he is a psychopath. Killers have *evaded the police, if only a few. Jack The Ripper. The Zodiac Killer. Others whom no one knows. How many unsolved murders take place in a year?*

If Luke's a psychopath, is he betting that he's smarter than anyone else? Does he think he won't be caught?

Here, in my mansion, I can think these thoughts without needing to push them away. Here, if nowhere else.

So, what do I do? I'm heading to the Surgeon's house, yet I'm inside my mind, focusing on Luke Titan.

What do I know? John Presley's murder doesn't match the others. That's a fact. He died after speaking to Veronica Lopez about Luke. Veronica Lopez went missing shortly after talking to me.

Did Luke kill Presley, mimicking the Surgeon? If he did, what does that have to do with the Surgeon? It's a separate crime, yet I'm here instead of in his room.

Those are the questions I've been avoiding.

What has Luke done on this case, truthfully? Nothing. No great breaks. He works a lot of hours, but in those hours, what is he accomplishing? Neither Tommy nor I have noticed because we've been preoccupied, but it's true. Tommy worked the angles I gave him, but Luke has offered very little.

The question I need to answer tonight is what connection exists between Luke and Bradley Brown?

<h1 style="text-align:center">CHAPTER THIRTY</h1>

Christian opened his eyes and saw Bradley Brown's street.

"How long have we been here?" he asked.

"Fifteen minutes," Tommy replied. Christian didn't look at him but could see Tommy staring from across the car. "What just happened?"

"I went to my mansion. I needed to put some pieces together. I'd been ignoring it for too long and missing things."

"Well, did you put them together?" Tommy asked.

"Some."

"Care to share?"

It was time to allow Tommy to hear this theory, which seemed insane in the bright light of reality.

No, Melissa said. Christian didn't turn around, though he heard her voice from the back seat. *Not yet. If you tell him now, he won't believe you. You'll isolate and ostracize yourself because you have nothing but the book inside your head.*

"Later," Christian replied. "We need to get into Brown's house, though. Now, not later."

Tommy's brow furrowed. "What?"

"I don't know if something is happening, but I think it might be. There's too much pressure on this situation. Brown is feeling it, and we are too. Whatever we need, whatever evidence exists, it's inside that house, and we have to get to it."

"I don't think you understand the point of a stakeout. It's to observe. If we go up to his front door right now, all that blows up. We can't observe him anymore. And it's two in the fucking morning, Christian, in case you didn't notice."

Christian swallowed. He knew all that, but he also remembered what he had read in the book. *The question I need to answer tonight is what connection exists between Luke and Bradley Brown?*

Tonight, not tomorrow. Now, not later. Christian never questioned what he found in the mansion. He trusted it implicitly because it never let him down. If the book said he needed to figure it out tonight, then tonight was what mattered. Not listening wasn't even possible, even if he wanted to. Christian had spent too many years following his mind's directions to go against it now.

No, Tommy was wrong. They weren't here tonight to observe. They were here to solve this damned thing.

Christian opened his car door without another word. He stepped outside and jogged across the street, not looking back to see if Tommy was following.

"Christian!" Tommy's voice was a harsh whisper that didn't echo but reached Christian's ears all the same. Christian said nothing but kept jogging, moving across the neighbors' lawns.

He stopped when he reached Brown's. He stood underneath a streetlight for everyone to see him. Should he sneak around the back, looking in windows, playing a sleuth? Or should he go right to the front door and force the issue?

Tonight. Not tomorrow. Not the next day.

Christian walked across the yard and up to the front door. He could hear Tommy's feet hitting the pavement behind him, on his way to back up a partner he must feel was insane.

Christian rang the doorbell.

Maybe everyone involved in this was insane.

Luke heard the doorbell.

It meant Christian had made his move. Certainly, Tommy would never have marched up to the house during a stakeout, and no one else would be here at this hour. No, Christian Windsor had figured it out or was on his way to doing so.

Luke thought that was simply remarkable. No fear or panic entered his mind. He stood in the same position as the doorbell's ring faded, though Mr. Brown turned around at a speed that could have injured his ankles. Mr. Ranger stared at the door, too, hope blooming on his face.

Luke looked at the two men, understanding coming to him. Christian's move forced the issue, but that was fine. Luke's plans were long and complex, encompassing many different pathways, and if this was the one Fate forced him down, then he would meet it with a smile. No grim determination rested inside him, only playfulness.

Because this, above all else, would be fun.

"Who the fuck is that?" Mr. Brown asked.

"I think it's my partners."

"You told them I was here? You *fucking* told them!" Mr. Brown said, whipping around.

"No, of course not. Remember, they've been following you. However, one of my partners is a savant, and I think he's figured out what's going on."

"What the fuck are you talking about?"

Luke straightened, no longer leaning on the counter. He walked over to Mr. Ranger's wheelchair and stepped behind it.

"I think Agent Christian Windsor has an inkling that we're working together, or at least that a connection exists that shouldn't."

"So, what do we do?" Mr. Brown spat.

"Isn't that obvious? We kill them."

Bradley's left hand shook as he stood in front of the front door. He had looked through the peephole a moment before and saw Titan was right. Two men stood there, the two from the day before. The younger one in front had to be Christian Windsor, the savant who had figured everything out.

Bradley didn't know if he believed a goddamn word Titan said, but his left hand was shaking so badly he couldn't think of anything else to do.

We kill them, Titan had said.

He made it sound so goddamn easy. Just off two FBI agents who showed up at his house this early in the morning.

Bradley could hear his mother calling from the back, the doorbell having woken her. Titan better fucking deal with her, though he better not hurt her. Not a hair on her head.

The doorbell rang again, and Bradley jumped backward a step. He looked down at his left hand and shoved it into his pocket.

"Fine, motherfuckers. Fine."

He reached forward and opened the door, a look of concern donning his face as the two men came into view.

"Hello?" he said, hoping his voice carried just the right amount of annoyance.

"Hi, Mr. Brown," Christian Windsor said. "I was in the neighborhood and wanted to talk with you if you had the time."

"Do you *know* what fucking *time* it is?"

"Yeah, I'm sorry about coming at this hour, but it's pretty important we talk."

Remember what you're supposed to do. Don't turn them away. Kill them.

Bradley looked at the agent behind Windsor, the older one. He wasn't looking at Bradley but at his partner. *He didn't want to be here.*

Windsor is calling the shots right now. Titan wasn't lying about that, Bradley thought.

"Whatever," he said. "Come on in."

He moved away from the door, opening his house to

them. Windsor walked in, followed by the other one; Bradley couldn't remember his name. Couldn't remember much because the front of his head was starting to fucking hurt again. Always at the worst time. Always trying to steal things from him, just like the rest of the goddamn world.

He closed his eyes tight for a second, trying to force away the pain. He couldn't hold them like that, though, not with the two goddamn cops here. He opened his eyes to see them both staring at him. The door was still ajar.

"Are you okay?" the older agent asked.

"Besides the fact that you two are here after I just worked a long shift? Yeah, I'm peachy." He turned and closed the door. "Let's go to the kitchen."

He led the way, hoping Titan wasn't lying. Ranger had better be back in one of the rooms, as well as his mother, quiet but not harmed. Titan had better be hiding, too.

How has it all gotten so fucked up? he wondered.

Shut up. You've got work to do and sitting here worrying about your problems isn't going to get any of it done.

Christian moved to where Titan had stood and leaned against the counter in the same spot.

"I'd offer you two a seat, but I don't want you to get comfortable. Now, what do you want?"

Windsor was looking around the kitchen in much the same fashion a hound dog would use his nose—as if he knew a clue rested in this place, and once he saw it, everything would be solved. Bradley didn't look around even though he wanted to. He had to trust Titan.

"Hello?" Bradley snapped. "You like my interior decorating? Want to talk about that?"

"I'm sorry," the older agent replied. "We, um—"

"I'd like to talk about your father," Windsor interrupted as if he hadn't heard his partner. He met Bradley's eyes. "Can we discuss how he died?"

Bradley's jaw involuntarily flexed. "I don't like remembering it."

"You don't like remembering it, or you don't want to talk about what actually happened?"

"You don't know what you're fucking talking about." The rage in his voice was real now, no longer a ploy to cover the panic.

"I do, and you know I do. What was the final straw, Bradley? What made you decide you had to kill him? That there wasn't any other way?"

Bradley shook his head. He hadn't thought about it in a long time. He and his mother never mentioned it after he took her eyes. Nothing that happened in the past was mentioned in *his* house now.

"I didn't kill him."

"You did, though. How did you learn to take eyes out so carefully? With so much attention to detail?"

Bradley shook his head again, but he didn't say anything.

"Was it the animals? It was, wasn't it? You started there, using the traps on your farm. You'd take their eyes out before skinning them. Your parents didn't know because when you brought the animal in to be eaten, it was fully dressed. Was your father the first *person's* eyes you took?"

Bradley looked through his tears, barely keeping them from spilling over onto his cheeks.

"What did he do to you?" the agent asked.

"How do you know?" Bradley finally whispered.

Windsor said nothing, only stared at him. Bradley felt he saw everything. He couldn't hide from that all-encompassing stare. Those eyes were what his father had wanted from his mother and him. Those eyes were truth, more so than any of the ones Bradley had collected so far.

As a tear fell from Bradley, a tall, dark figure appeared behind the two agents. It moved with no more substance than a shadow, not a sound creaking out from beneath its feet as it flashed over the two agents.

A hand came down, and the older one collapsed to the floor.

The perfect eyes, the ones holding the truth, grew alarmed as their owner tried to turn around. Windsor couldn't because that same blazing quick hand came down. Bradley saw that it held a gun that pistol-whipped the back of Windsor's head.

Both agents lay on Bradley's floor. Luke Titan stood above them, smiling. "Should we get started?"

Veronica's eyes hurt.

She didn't remember anyone removing the blindfold, but brightness fell down on her like heaven had opened its gates, shining on all the evil to ever exist.

She clenched them shut as hands grabbed her. She felt her arms being untied, but before she could move them, they were pushed down to her naked stomach and retied there.

Veronica cried out, opening her eyes wide, but she only

saw an outline above her. The light behind the person masked their face's details.

"Please," she pleaded.

Her legs were worked on with the same efficiency, then a bag was shoved over her head, blinding her as the light had done but with less pain.

Hands lifted her off the bed. Despite everything happening, her mind registered how easily they moved her as if she was no more than a loose sheet of paper. She felt the change in the air as she exited the room. Going somewhere, and dear God, was this it? Would she be raped and murdered now? For days she'd laid inside that room, thinking it would come soon, but it hadn't. She'd been left alone for the most part, and her mind must have begun to think it wouldn't happen.

But it was.

Veronica screamed or tried, but her voice was a whisper. She hadn't spoken in so long that her vocal cords had forgotten how to work.

"Shhh," a voice cautioned.

She felt a couch underneath her.

There were lips next to her ears, and a voice said, "Don't move."

Please God, she prayed. *Please don't let this happen. Please.*

She felt a rag cover her face, and before she could hold her breath, she had inhaled whatever substance it held.

CHAPTER THIRTY-ONE

Luke looked at the five people in front of him. Christian and Tommy lay head to foot on the floor, still unconscious from Luke's ferocious strike. Ms. Lopez lay on the couch, the chloroform having done its job. Mr. Ranger occupied his wheelchair, the only victim still allowed to look around because of his inability to tell the world anything.

And Bradley Brown stood in front of all of it.

"I said I would help you, Mr. Brown, and so I have. Here they are, everyone you need to ensure your safety moving forward. I will, of course, clean up from my end. The bureau will not know your name. I will create evidence that points to someone else. You'll be safe, but you must leave. You and your mother. You will move to Canada, not stay in the States, since I know you can't control yourself now. You will start up again, and my record is far too pristine to have collared the wrong person when you're eventually caught."

Mr. Brown didn't turn as Luke spoke. He stared in disbelief at what Luke had given him, a gift that he'd never seen before. Perfection, for someone like him, lay before him.

"If you don't leave the country, I *will* call on you, Mr. Brown. I *will* kill you. Do you understand?"

The man nodded.

"Good. I will leave you to it, then. When you're finished, pack and go to Canada. I will make sure nothing that happens here points to you. Okay?"

Another nod. Luke knew the man wasn't lying. He had seen Luke's hand and knew it was at least as powerful as God's. He knew that Luke only spoke truth, and what he said would happen.

Luke turned from the room and left the five people to the chaos that he'd created for them.

***

Christian dreamed not of Luke but of a monster. Monsters create monsters, just as humans spawn humans. Bradley Brown had to come from somewhere, and since Christian had refused to watch the video his mind had prepared, it forced it upon him during his unconsciousness.

The room Christian stands in is dark, but it always is when these things happen to Bradley Brown. Because the monster doesn't want to see his act, he wants to see something else.

There's grunting across the room and the sound of a bed squeaking. The grunting comes from the monster's mouth, and though he's not a man, he is male.

Christian steps closer to the bed, knowing that it

wouldn't matter even if he sat down on it. These people cannot see him.

A flashlight turns on, and Christian sees more. A woman is bent over, naked, and the monster is behind her. She has a ball gag in her mouth, but this isn't a BDSM sex game. This is rape, pure and simple. The monster is pounding ruthlessly, and the light shines on the woman's face.

"LOOK AT ME!"

The woman does because she knows that if she doesn't, worse pain will come. Much worse.

"Yes," the monster moans.

Christian glances at the woman's eyes only for a second because he can't handle any more than that. Her face is twisted in pain, fear, and hate. Hair falls across it, but the monster reaches forward and pushes it away, making sure he can see her eyes. The hatred—at life, at this man, at herself—bleeds from them.

The light moves and shines on a boy. He's in his early teens, and if hate lived in the woman's eyes, hell's fire rages in his. He's naked, tied, and ball-gagged too. The light shines on the boy as the monster dismounts the woman.

He moves to the boy, and despite being bound, the child kicks, trying to keep the monster away. The monster is strong, though, and with a few punches to the face, the boy is subdued. He lays on his stomach and the monster has his way with him next, the light intermittently flashing from the boy's face to the woman's.

The room fades to black, then Christian is in a kitchen —the one he saw years ago when the boy didn't bring back the trapped animal. He knows time has passed because the decorations have changed.

"You motherfucker! You goddamn motherfucker! I'm going to kill you!"

Christian hears the words but can't see who is speaking. He moves around the kitchen's island and walks into the connected dining room. Now he sees. The monster is bound to the table, thick ropes around his legs, arms, torso, and neck. The large wooden table gives the monster six inches on either side of his head and feet. Spit flecks his face from the words he screams into the empty dining room.

Christian hears steps and looks to his left.

The dining room is no longer empty.

The boy is nearly a man now, and he's holding a small leather bag.

He moves to the table and says nothing to the monster, simply begins laying out tools from inside the bag. A scalpel. A spoon-like apparatus. Other things Christian hasn't seen but understands.

The boy gets to work on the monster, leaving him awake as he does. Screams and blood fill the room but no help comes, and eventually, the screams die to whimpers. Finally, there is silence, and the boy steps back. Blood covers his hands and arms. It has splattered on his face.

The body in front of him has large round holes where the monster's eyeballs should be. The bloody orbs are next to his left arm, one looking at the boy's chest and the other at the ceiling.

The dining room fades to black. Christian is in the farm's fields next. He knows what happens here. He can see the heap of the monster's body lying a hundred feet in front of him. The boy sits in a tractor that harvests crops, and as he starts moving it forward, Christian wishes he could turn away.

The boy is now another monster.

Bradley looked at the four people, frightened of what had been given to him. He still didn't fully understand how it all happened, but here they were, all ready for whatever he fancied.

Bradley cleared his throat and looked at Charlie.

"I need to wake the rest up. I think I'd like everyone awake when I get started."

Bradley walked over to Christian Windsor and slapped his face. The man stirred and Bradley slapped him again, bringing him out of his slumber. Bradley said nothing but moved to the older agent and roughly slapped him until he woke.

Finally, he went to the woman. He didn't slap her but shook her. It took longer, but eventually, she came to.

Everyone was awake.

"Listen to me," the older agent said. "Whatever you're thinking, you don't want to do it."

Bradley turned from the couch and looked at the bound man on the floor. He smiled. "Why don't I?"

"Because you're going to get caught. Our other partner is supposed to take over our watch soon, and when he can't get in touch with us, it's over for you."

Bradley's smile widened. He couldn't say anything,

though, not if he wanted to keep living after this night. "I'll take my chances. Excuse me for a bit. I have to go grab some things."

Bradley moved through the house to his room. He fleetingly thought about checking in on his mother, but the fever was on him now, and he couldn't pull himself away from the living room for too long. No, he'd check her later. Right now, he needed to start cutting.

He grabbed his little bag that held all the necessary tools and rushed out of his bedroom.

"Okay, I'm sorry," he said as he entered the living room. Everyone was in the same spots, but the conversation stopped when they saw him. "What were you talking about?"

"I asked them who you are and what you want," the woman explained.

"Did they tell you?"

"You're the Surgeon."

"I suppose that'll work," Bradley said. He really did like the name. It lent an air of prestige and importance to what he was doing, even if no one in the room understood it except Windsor. He seemed to know more than he should, and if he started talking, Bradley would end him first. Whatever it took to get him to shut up.

"Listen!" the older agent said. "You have to let us go, or our partner *will* find you."

Bradley ignored him and walked over to Charlie. He picked the old man up and tossed him on the floor. Bradley took the rope out of his bag and quickly bound Charlie's arms and legs, though he didn't think the geriatric would put up much of a fight.

"I'm going to start with you, Charlie. I want to be fresh when I cut on you. It's hard work, but I'm sure you know that since you were a doctor. By the end, you're exhausted."

Bradley grabbed his bag and knelt on the floor. He pulled out his wire speculum and attached the holds to Charlie's eyelids, ensuring that he wouldn't be able to blink during what came next.

"It's not your fault."

The voice came from the other side of the room. Bradley didn't need to turn to know who had spoken. Christian Windsor.

Bradley kept pulling out his tools, trying to ignore the nonsense the man spouted.

"Do you hear me, Bradley? It's not your fault. None of this. You... At least some part of you was forced to do this."

Bradley stopped laying his tools down. "Shut up."

"I know what happened," the agent continued. "I know what your father did to you and your mother."

"You don't know any-fucking-thing." Bradley's jaw tightened, muscles flexing up the side of his face.

"I do. I know about the abuse. I know why you wanted his eyes."

Bradley looked down and saw his left hand shaking. He needed both to pull out Charlie's goddamn eyes. This motherfucker had to shut up if Bradley was going to be able to do anything here.

"Shut your mouth," he snapped.

"You want the truth from people," the agent added. "The truth your father always said was in people's eyes. But you never found truth with him or your mother, not the truth you needed. It's the same truth we all need, Bradley. Love. That's why you're doing this, isn't it?"

Bradley stood without knowing he was doing it and looked at the bound agent. "If you don't stop talking, I'll kill you first." His words were calm and measured despite the rage building inside him. "You don't know anything about me or what I went through, and you don't know anything about why I do this. You're not smart enough to know or deep enough to understand. Do you get that?"

Bradley said the words, but his eyes met the agent's, and he felt weak. An empathy he didn't know was possible lay within them. An empathy he'd wanted from his parents, from friends, from *anyone*...and never found.

Bradley knew what to do. He grabbed the tools that lay next to Charlie and brought them over to Christian Windsor. He'd start with the agent.

***

Luke sat in his car a half-mile down the street. The dashboard clock told him ten minutes had passed, and he was curious about what was happening inside.

He watched the clock tick another minute off. Time always marched forward, and in the human consciousness, everyone saw it as another minute closer to their death. Time revolved around each individual person, and each minute was one that was solely theirs. The fact that the universe continued its expansion and would keep on going until all the stars and planets died, leaving only a cold, still, and silent reality for everyone. Well, they didn't think of *that* when a minute passed. It wasn't the universe's extinction they considered, but their own.

Luke recognized that truth as he watched the clock, though he was thinking selfishly as well. What he had done here had been good but not great. Not nearly what he'd wanted to accomplish, and each passing minute chipped away at his ability to perform that great act. The greatness he wanted relied on Christian Windsor. The boy had been a blessing, his intelligence combined with his handicaps. Luke couldn't have asked for a better addition to his plans.

Yet, he'd given Windsor up early. His eyes would be removed, and even if Mr. Brown left him alive, he wouldn't be involved with Luke any longer. No more FBI for Mr. Windsor, not once Mr. Brown finished with him.

Luke looked out the car's front window. Did he want to let the two live? Would that be more fun in the long term, or was Windsor too close to the truth? If Luke let him die, he could restart his plans. Would a longer timeline be more fun?

So many questions and not much time to decide on the answers.

Christian looked at the metal contraptions, many of them the same ones he had seen in his dream. He wasn't surprised since his mind didn't lead him astray, even down to the details.

"Stop fucking talking," Tommy snarled from Christian's feet.

Christian ignored him. All he could do was talk. It was

his only weapon against Bradley Brown. He was clearly hitting nerves, but not the right ones. He needed to say something to break the man down, to bring him back to the childlike state the monster had ruled over. Only that would slow this massacre down.

But to what end? Melissa asked. *You can slow him down, but you're still tied up without anywhere to go. Eventually, he'll get started again.*

Christian saw her standing behind Brown, but he didn't look at her because her words didn't matter, not right now. Slow Brown down first, then worry about what to do next.

"You don't have to do this," Christian whispered as the man knelt in front of him. "You didn't deserve for those things to happen to you. It wasn't your fault, and you don't have to keep doing this. You can stop it right now."

He watched without moving as Brown attached the apparatus he used on the old man. Christian's eyes were held open, and he stared at Brown as the man put the rest of the tools on the floor as a surgeon might do.

"*STOP!*" Veronica shrieked hoarsely from the couch. Christian heard her trying to free herself. He pushed her from his mind, focusing only on the man above him.

"You don't need my eyes to be loved, Bradley."

The man was holding a scalpel, but he stopped moving. "You don't know anything, so shut up. Just shut the fuck up."

Christian said nothing for a second, and Brown started moving again. He brought the scalpel down to Christian's eye. He could see the blade, large like a huge metal god, ready to deliver its unbending judgment.

He felt the blade cut into his eye—a small incision, but

blood spurted onto Christian's cheek. He gasped. "Bradley, don't. Don't keep this going. Let your father die by not killing us."

Brown paused, tears filling his eyes.

"He *can* die," Christian pressed. "You can kill him forever by stopping now."

Brown shook his head but said nothing. Tears rolled down his face.

Christian saw movement behind Brown, and he followed it. Brown saw him looking and turned his head to see over his shoulder.

Luke pointed a gun at the man's skull from a distance of two feet.

He pulled the trigger, and Bradley Brown's head exploded in a mess of blood, bone, and brain.

CHAPTER THIRTY-TWO

Luke followed the nurse into the common area. He had told her that he was here to follow up on Charles Ranger, to make sure he was doing okay and see if there was anything the FBI could do to help his recovery.

"That's very, very kind of you, Mr. Titan," the nurse said after checking his credentials.

She walked him down the hallway, telling him that it had been a very frightening experience for Mr. Ranger and that the old man was having trouble sleeping. They, of course, had therapy on site for him, and with a little bit of time, they thought he would be okay. Therapy was tough for him, though, given his inability to speak.

"It takes longer," she said.

Luke thought that Mr. Ranger wouldn't need any more therapy once he finished here.

The old man sat in his wheelchair, the television on in front of him and four other "guests."

"Betty, would you mind giving Charles some space?

This gentleman would like to speak with him," the nurse said.

The woman looked at Luke. He smiled at her.

"Oh, yes, sure. Charles, we'll talk later, okay?" The old woman bustled off through the room.

"Thank you, ma'am," Luke told the nurse. "I'll check in with you before I leave, okay?"

"Sure thing, Agent Titan. Charles, this man is from the FBI to check up on you. He's the one that saved your life, right?"

Charles Ranger didn't nod or shake his head. He stared with wide eyes and not a drop of color in his face.

"Probably surprised to see you." The nurse smiled once more at Luke and walked off down the hall.

Luke pulled up a chair directly in front of Mr. Ranger. A week had passed since Luke decided he wanted Christian Windsor to live a bit longer. He wanted to see how much he could do with Mr. Windsor before the boy needed to pass from this planet.

"Hi, Mr. Ranger. How are you?"

The old man only stared, his mouth open as if he might start drooling at any second.

"I wanted to come by and talk to you for a minute. I know you're in therapy, but I'm guessing you haven't mentioned what happened in Mr. Brown's house. Is that right?"

No sign from Mr. Ranger.

"I'm going to need a nod before I continue. Nod if you haven't said anything."

The old man nodded.

"Good. You're a smart man. You must be smart to end up in a place as nice as this one. You were a doctor, right?"

Another nod.

"Yes, you're definitely smart, so I know that you'll keep quiet about what went on the other night. If you don't, well, I'd hate to have to come visit you again since it won't be as pleasant. Do you understand? Nod again if you do."

Mr. Ranger did as he requested.

"That's good." Luke patted the old man's knee. "I'm going to get out of here, then. I just wanted to make sure we were on the same page moving forward. As long as you keep your word, you'll never see me again. In the end, I did you a favor, didn't I? I got rid of Mr. Brown."

He smiled.

Veronica walked into Luke Titan's office. She watched the FBI agent stand behind his desk and smile. Veronica's hands were shaking.

"Hi, Ms. Lopez. How are you doing?"

Veronica looked at her feet and felt hot tears fill her eyes. "I'm okay."

"Come, have a seat." Titan moved out from behind his desk and pulled the chair out, motioning to her.

Veronica listened to him without saying anything, trying to hold herself together. She didn't want to cry in here, but that was a foolish thing to think, really. She had come to apologize and thank him, this man who she'd been out to prove as some kind of criminal but had ended up saving her life.

"I, uh," she began as Titan took his seat. "I wanted to say I'm sorry. I wanted to say it in person." She looked up at Titan. "I was completely wrong, and I felt you needed to hear it from me."

"It's no problem, Ms. Lopez. No apology needed. Apparently, Bradley Brown was obsessed with me, and the things he did would have made anyone think I was involved. Especially after John Presley. I'm just glad I made it there in time."

Veronica nodded, unsure of what to say next.

"Are you going to continue writing the book about the Sphere?"

"I am, but I'm taking a break for a little while. Maybe in six months."

"That makes sense," Titan agreed. "You went through a harrowing experience. Time off is exactly what I'd recommend if I were your doctor."

"Do you..." Veronica didn't know why she was about to ask the question, but it flew out of her mouth before she could stop herself. "Do you still practice?"

"Therapy?"

"Yes."

"I haven't in a while. Why?"

"I don't know. I just... I haven't found a doctor I like yet."

"It's only been three weeks," Titan said.

"I know, but... You were there. I trust you." Veronica laughed and wiped tears from her eyes. "I know, it's crazy. Forget I asked."

Titan was quiet for a moment while Veronica looked at her feet, feeling stupid for investigating him, somehow getting herself caught by a serial killer, and now asking him if he'd take her on as a patient. She felt lost, groveling to the man she had once thought should be jailed.

"I think I have the time to take on a patient. My license is still active. When are you free?"

Homage was paid by the entire FBI. Senior officials came to Luke's office and sent emails, and he was scheduled to receive an award for outstanding work later this week. Luke played the role expected of him, humble and thankful he could be of service.

None of the praise or awards mattered to him. He put up with them because they were necessary if he were to keep going forward, which after the decision he made weeks ago, was imperative.

It was Friday night around seven, and Luke saw Tommy walking across the mostly empty floor. He stuck his head in Luke's office.

"Want to grab a drink?"

"I think I'm going to head home tonight. Pretty tired."

Tommy smiled. "All those bigwigs wearing you out, huh?"

"It's a lot," Luke said, smiling back.

"You deserve it, and even if you don't, I still want them to give you the keys to the city. Saved my life, man. Thanks again."

Luke had called Tommy's phone twice before he re-entered Bradley Brown's house. He called Christian's once as well, receiving no answer from either. The official story said he'd shown up to relieve them from their shift a bit early because they'd both worked a double with Christian's training. He arrived, saw their empty car, and saved the day.

That had been a risk, though Luke had known when he walked back in that he needn't worry about it. Had either of the two shown recognition or fear when he returned to the house, Luke would've killed them both. Neither of them remembered even *entering* the home, however. The blow Luke had delivered to Tommy kept him from remembering anything before they exited the car, and Christian didn't remember anything after ringing the doorbell.

"If you keep thanking me, next time, I won't save you." Luke still had a smile on his face.

"All right. Windsor comes back Monday. He's tougher than I thought. You should have seen him in there. He somehow talked enough to keep Brown from killing the old man and himself. I don't know how long he could have kept it up, but he was hitting some tough body shots on that motherfucker."

"Yeah, I wasn't sure in the beginning, but I'm glad he's here," Luke said.

"Okay. See ya Monday."

Tommy left the office, and Luke was alone again. He watched his partner walk across the floor and wondered when he'd have his next opportunity to kill the man.

CHAPTER THIRTY-THREE

Christian took about a month off after the final altercation with Brown. Waverly had said he could have more time if he wanted, but he found himself desiring to get back to work.

"Thought you never wanted to be in the field?" Waverly asked when Christian told him.

"I know. It's the people I work with, I think."

"You're with the best," Waverly had said.

Christian's eye was mostly healed, though it had itched like crazy when the doctor first stitched him up.

He'd seen Melissa multiple times per week during his time off.

"So, what do you think of him now?" she asked him.

"Of Luke?"

"Yes, is he a savior or a villain in your mind?"

Christian spent much of the past month thinking about that. His mind had told him to find the connection between Brown and Luke that very night, but the connection ended up being a bullet from Luke's gun to Brown's brain.

He had never denied his mind what it wished to tell him, but now, reality said that he was wrong for the first time.

"He's a savior," Christian told Melissa. "A lot of the connections I made were because Brown was trailing Luke. Presley's death. Veronica going missing. It makes sense now, though it didn't before. I tried to understand the connections, but they never fully fit."

"That's good, Christian," Melissa said. "There are a lot of things wrong in the world, but this Luke Titan guy seems to be good for it. For you too."

Now, Christian knocked on Luke's door, his first time at the office since Luke had shot off Bradley Brown's face.

"Come in," he heard from inside.

Christian opened the door.

"Hello," Luke said with a broad smile. "Heard you were coming back today. How are you feeling?"

"I'm a lot better. The eye still itches some, but nothing too bad."

"Good, because we have a lot of work for you to get started on."

Christian smiled back. He wanted something to take his mind off the past month's thoughts.

"I appreciate you both coming to the hospital. I'm sorry I haven't called since I got out," Christian said. "I just really wanted some separation from this place. Thank you for what you did, Luke. You saved my life."

"Too many thanks have been given over this already. I

have that silly ceremony today where they'll drape a medal on my chest, and I'm not looking forward to it. Can I say, 'you're welcome' once, and we let this go? Move on to the next case?"

Christian smiled. "If that's what you want."

"It is. You're welcome."

"The ceremony is at noon?" Christian asked.

"That's what they tell me. Are you coming?"

"Of course. Wouldn't look good if the people you saved didn't show up."

"I *am* all about appearances," Luke replied. "Have a seat?"

Christian did, and both were silent for a few seconds.

"Was that the first person you killed?" Christian asked, quickly realizing how it might sound. "I mean, as an FBI agent."

Luke smiled. "Yes, first one."

"Do you think about it still?"

"About killing Bradley Brown?"

Christian nodded.

"No. At least not in the way you probably mean. I don't dwell on the physics of his death."

"I think about it," Christian said. "I think about the way his head exploded and the colors everything inside it made."

"Why?"

"I don't know. I've never seen anyone die."

Luke nodded. "It reminds us of our own mortality. That we're all really just meat and blood, with a false layer of consciousness overlaid."

"False?"

"The Buddhists would tell you if it exists, then point to it. You can't."

Christian looked down at his lap. "I'll probably have to kill someone. I don't want to."

"Not if they kill you first," Luke said and then laughed. "Come on. Let's get lunch before the ceremony."

Christian stood and walked out of the office with Luke Titan. They seemed like the best of friends.

FOR CHRISTIAN WINDSOR

Christian,

I am not sure when you'll receive this letter, but I am certain it will reach you one day. I think you're going to allow me to really push myself over the coming years, so I decided to keep you alive.

I think I'll give you this letter when it's too late for you. When you finally realize you're going to die, and nothing can be done. That would make me happy.

How close were you this time to understanding my true nature? I feel that if you'd had a bit more time, things might have turned out very differently for everyone involved, though perhaps not for Bradley Brown. His loss, though, was our gain. You and I have a long way to go, but in the end, I think you'll see my purpose. I think you'll see it, and I think it will terrify you.

The day you receive this letter is the day you have recognized it.

I can't wait.
All the best,
Luke Titan

M.D., Ph.D., Special Agent for the Federal Bureau of Investigations

---

You've started the journey. Get a step closer to finishing it in *The Priest's Fire.*

Did you like this book? If so, please leave an awesome review! As an independent author, reviews are always extremely helpful!

Review Here!

PREVIEW OF THE PRIEST'S FIRE

Lucy Speckle stared at the television. Her attention focused entirely on it, not noticing the small tics that broke out across her face from time to time. The people around her didn't notice either, but it wasn't because they were focused on the TV like Lucy. They had … other issues.

"We are here today to commemorate an FBI agent whose name many of you probably already know. His accomplishments are nearly legend, and we are all lucky to have him helping keep our citizens safe. We'd like to present Luke Titan with our highest award…"

Lucy didn't know the man speaking, and she didn't care about him. He was *nonessential.* Lucy believed heavily in the essential and the nonessential. Anything that didn't fit into the first bucket could be discarded without further thought, and in Lucy's mind, there was only a single *essential* guiding force: the one true God of Abraham and Isaac.

Yet, despite the *non-essentialness* of the man speaking, she couldn't pull herself away from the screen. She wasn't looking at *him*, though, or the person he appeared to be speaking *about*.

Lucy watched someone on the back left. His hands were folded in front of him, and he looked uncomfortable in his suit and tie. To Lucy Speckle, it was clear he didn't want to be on stage.

"Who is that?" Lucy asked, her voice snapping out across the room's silence. Her normal stutter was missing.

"Lucy, please stay calm," someone nonessential said from her side. For the most part, all the people who worked here were nonessential. They didn't serve God but the government, an evil organization Lucy had no time for. She knew God would get her out of this wretched place sooner or later. He had put her here for a reason, and if she didn't understand why yet, she trusted Him implicitly.

But now, staring at the television screen, perhaps she'd found the reason—the man standing on stage to the left. How long had the preacher spoken about this moment? For how many years had her and Daddy—and Momma, though to a lesser degree—prayed for worthiness and to be shown what Lucy now saw?

"Who is that?" She stood, ignoring the orderly next to her, and walked to the television, placing her hand directly on the man. "Who is he?" She looked around the room, but she saw only blank faces. "What is his name?"

Lucy was growing angry at these people, the fact that no one would answer her.

"His name is Christian Windsor," an orderly said. Three more nonessentials had come into the room, ready to calm Lucy Speckle if she couldn't do it herself. "He's an FBI agent."

That was all she needed. Lucy stepped back from the television and stared at Christian Windsor. Even the name seemed...*Godly*.

Her right eyebrow twitched upward and her head jerked down before regaining its usual place. Lucy didn't notice.

She stared at the screen until the ceremony ended and the next show started. Only then did she break her concentration.

Lucy walked to a corner in the large room and found a chair away from everyone else. She sat and thought about the man on TV.

The next few weeks were turbulent for Lucy. She often found herself angry at those around her, which meant she ended up in one of those jackets that wouldn't let her move. They called it a straitjacket. She called it "fucking bullshit," one of the few times Lucy Speckle used such language, then she spat at the orderlies who put it on her. God didn't like curse words, but Daddy used them when he was mad, though he always repented.

They were nonessentials, but she still couldn't help the anger she felt toward them. She shouldn't be in here, not with all the rest of these crazies. She didn't know how long she had been here. She hadn't been good at keeping up with time since Daddy died, but now that she had seen Christian Windsor, she knew she'd been here *too* long.

No one ever visited her, and that was more than fine. She didn't want to talk with anyone. Not her family, though they had all pretty much disowned Daddy decades ago. Lucy never really had any friends. She didn't need any besides God, and He was always with her.

Those weeks were awful, especially when locked away inside the straitjacket because she felt God trying to speak, but she couldn't hear Him well inside this place. It was like the walls were built with a material that kept God out. Lucy knew that couldn't possibly be true, that the God of Abraham did whatever He wanted when He wanted.

Perhaps the walls simply interfered with *her* ability to hear Him. That made more sense.

Either way, the result was the same. Lucy knew that the person she had seen on the television screen, *Christian Windsor*, was the one her and Daddy—actually, the whole church—had been searching for, but she wanted confirmation.

Finally, Lucy had quit fighting the orderlies and doctors that came around. Just as she had realized years ago how nonessential the kids mocking her at school were, she understood that fighting these nonessentials was keeping God at bay. So, she lay down on her bed and quit caring about this ephemeral world, which was only a test from God and one she had to rise above.

She urinated and defecated on herself during this time. Her eyes never left the ceiling. She didn't move when the orderlies came to change her clothes, her arms and legs pliable as they undressed and redressed her. Only a few more hours would pass before more bodily functions occurred, and the orderlies had to do it all again. She didn't care. Truthfully, she didn't even notice. Lucy had gone to

God. For once, she was able to do it without the instruments Daddy had given her.

God was talking to *her*.

And in the end, it was glorious because Lucy finally understood that Daddy hadn't been lying all those years. They had been chosen, even if Daddy wasn't here to see it. The nonessential had fallen away for good, leaving room only for the essential.

And *that* was Christian Windsor. *He* was what God wanted for Lucy Speckle. What this whole hellish world had been about: to prepare her for him, God's Sword.

You've started the journey. Get a step closer to finishing it in *The Priest's Fire.*